Cover design by Elle Staples

Inside illustrations by Frank Nicholas

First published in 1953

This unabridged version has updated grammar and spelling.

© 2021 Jenny Phillips

goodandbeautiful.com

TABLE OF CONTENTS

CHAPTER 1 | Small Blue Canoe 1

CHAPTER 2 | Joe Meek Palavers 12

CHAPTER 3 | White-Headed Eagle 26

CHAPTER 4 | A Fight in the Grove 34

CHAPTER 5 | A Ship is Here 47

CHAPTER 6 | "Indians Stole Your Baby" 56

CHAPTER 7 | Tackett Begins a Search 65

CHAPTER 8 | The Old Tuality Trail 76

CHAPTER 9 | Grandfather Bear 82

CHAPTER 10 | Signal Smoke 89

CHAPTER 11 | Darkened Cabin 98

CHAPTER 12 | This Government Business 105

CHAPTER 13 | Wolf Meeting 114

CHAPTER 14 | Challenge at Champoeg 123

CHAPTER 1

Small Blue Canoe

A blue-stained Indian dugout slid silently through the hurrying water of the creek. The paddle dipped warily. Now it sent the canoe near the willow-lined shore; now it held poised on the sliding current.

The October sun scattered through the tangled willow and alder. It shone on the swinging black braids of the kneeling paddler and brought a glint to the color of the beads and ribbon. The only sound was an occasional splash from the clumsy oars of a skiff near the bend of the creek up ahead.

In the skiff, a big man in tattered buckskin narrowed his eyes and studied the screening bushes downstream. Joe Meek knew that he was being trailed. Someone in a canoe had been sneaking up the creek behind him ever since he'd turned from the Willamette River. He hadn't yet caught a glimpse of the craft. If he had been in the Rockies, where any Indian could be an enemy, he might have been alarmed. But Oregon Indians were peaceful, or had been, so far.

Being trailed in a boat was the thing that bothered him. Joe was a trapper, a "mountain man." Big-boned, long-legged, he could run faster than any Indian he'd ever met. He could shoot straighter than any man with whom he'd been matched. He could ride the wildest mountain pony ever roped. But almost anybody could handle a boat better than he could.

Try as he would to get used to the Oregon custom of traveling by boat, Joe still was uneasy without good solid earth under his feet. He would be at a disadvantage on the water if that was an enemy following him.

But who could the enemy be? One of the Hudson's Bay Company men? Had the British fur-trading company set someone to spy on him to see if he was trapping animals they claimed for their own? Were they following him merely because he was an American and active among the American settlers? Were they trying to get information about the settlers' meeting?

Joe Meek knew that the Company considered him a troublemaker, but he didn't think they took him seriously enough to set spies on his trail. Yet somebody in a canoe was after him, and somebody with a good heart wouldn't be likely to be so sly about it.

With sudden resolution, Joe Meek dug in an oar to turn his skiff to the bank. He caught up his gun and checked her priming. Then he stepped ashore and faded into the brush.

He was leaning on the overhanging limb of an alder when the blue canoe glided cautiously near the shore. He got a clear view of the young paddler intently watching the stream ahead. Then he chuckled with surprise. His "enemy" was an Indian girl, twelve or thirteen years old, fine in beads and white doeskin, high-laced moccasins, and ribbon-tied braids.

But she was following, all right. She caught sight of his skiff beached ahead and frowned and searched the shore with puzzled eyes.

Joe decided to give the girl a scare. "Lookin' for me, young 'un?" he shouted.

The girl jumped, so startled that she almost upset the canoe. Joe reached down with a big hand to steady it. The girl whirled, her braids swinging wildly, as she raised her paddle club-like. For a minute she looked wild as a forest animal, glaring at him. Then she let the paddle drop and sighed with relief.

"You are Joe Meek," she declared. "You are friend. Your wife is Indian woman, Nez Perce. I have been told you are a mighty hunter, a brave of great heart."

Joe cleared his throat and tried to look modest. He wondered how the girl knew so much about him. She talked nearly as good American as he did, so likely she came from Jason Lee's Mission back on the Willamette River. Twenty or thirty Indian youngsters boarded and studied there.

"I am named Keetow," she volunteered. "I thought it was you in that boat. I hoped you would lead me to the village of my people, the Chinooks."

Chinooks? That was a tribe living near the coast at the mouth of the Columbia River, more than a hundred miles away by water. Joe scowled doubtfully. "You ain't dressed like a Chinook," he said. "Only Horse Indian women wear clothes like you've got on."

She smoothed her doeskin skirt, pleased that Joe had noticed her pretty beaded dress. "My teacher at the Mission who has visited the Cayuse tribes helped me to sew it," she explained.

Joe pushed his broad-brimmed black hat to the back of his head. Plainly the youngster was running away. The missionaries wouldn't let a girl start out hunting for her tribe by herself when she didn't even know the way to go. Joe had a small half-Indian daughter at Marcus Whitman's Mission School in the Walla Walla country. He wouldn't like to think she'd run away, as this youngster was doing, traveling so bold in her little painted dugout canoe. He frowned at the figure of a fawn carved on the prow.

"Were they mean to you at the Mission?" he demanded.

Keetow shook her head. "Very kind. Very good."

"Then I reckon I'd better take you back."

She broke into cries of protest, part in English and part in an Indian tongue. She could not return to the Mission, she said. They were planning to send her on a great ship to the land of the white people. They wanted to show the Easterners how well she had learned at the Mission school.

Her teacher, Mrs. Garret, was going to take her in that ship. That was why the beautiful dress had been made. That was why she had been set to studying day and night to learn the language well. That was why she was running away.

She's plumb scared of the whole idea, thought Joe. And he wouldn't blame her. He would likely have been scared of such a trip himself at her age. Any youngster might shy at going around the Horn, six months at sea, then to be stared at by thousands of strangers.

Joe had been near eighteen when he skipped out from his Virginia home and headed for St. Louis on the edge of the frontier. He'd felt himself full-grown at eighteen. Even so, he'd been plenty uneasy.

But if he encouraged the girl in running away to the tribe, it would seem as if he were working against the people at the Mission. Joe wasn't a church-going man himself, but he admired the fine job Jason Lee was doing in Oregon. He not only taught the native Indians, but he also helped bring Americans here to settle. Jason Lee worked every way he could to bring settlers—American settlers—to the country.

Four years ago, in 1838, he had carried a petition for Territorial Government to Washington. When he made the trip East, he had taken three Indian boys from his Mission to show off to folks back home. The boys had done more to interest Congress in Oregon than any number of petitions.

But Keetow wouldn't understand that. She would only see that the three boys had not returned. That scared her, no doubt. It wouldn't be a matter easily explained.

As he studied the problem, the girl watched him with fawn-like staring eyes. Joe didn't rightly know what to do. Chinook village was a far ways off, and he had things to attend to down in this direction. He was on his way now to take word to Ambrose Brandt, up-creek a ways, about the settlers' meeting being called to "palaver" this government business.

It might be that Ambrose, for all he was a newcomer, would have an idea what to do with the young 'un. Ambrose was always stewing over what was right and wrong for his own two children, fourteen-year-old Tackett and that yellow-haired baby, Debbie. Their mother had been killed in a wagon accident on the trip west. That made Ambrose take family worries twice as hard as most men did.

Joe continued upstream in the direction he had been traveling. "Just keep a-followin'," he said. "There's some folks above might know how to help ye."

An hour or so later, Joe Meek helped the girl beach her canoe next to his skiff and led the way along a trampled path up to the Brandts' cabin.

The raw little cabin was set at one end of a clearing. To the side stretched a rough-plowed field with the wheat just stirring above ground. To the north, space had been fenced in to form a sort of corral, penning in a rangy, longhorned red cow and a newborn calf.

As Keetow followed Joe to the clearing, she saw a tall, black-bearded man and a reedy boy busily lashing willow poles to the corral fence. Nearby, on the muddy earth, a tow-headed baby girl played with some sticks and stones.

Joe Meek strode ahead, grinning from ear to ear. "By the great shaggy mountain," he shouted, "you're a farmer for sure, Ambrose. Now you got a cow!"

"She's Tackett's cow," the man called back, "providing, that is, that nobody claims her. The boy found her and brought her in a week ago."

Joe Meek laughed as he came striding forward. "I saw the 'found' notice you posted at the Trading House at Champoeg. You're bound to be lawful, ain't ye, Ambrose? Even in a land where there's no law!"

"The cow's got no brand on her," the boy put in hurriedly. "And anyhow, the calf belongs to me. It was born right here, and this here's American land."

Suddenly, Tackett Brandt stopped talking and stared wide-eyed at the Indian girl at Joe's heels.

Keetow was staring, too. She looked from one strange face to the other, from the little baby girl to the black-bearded man with sad, sunken eyes. Then her gaze took in Tackett's long hair, growing "mountain-man" style, his stubborn jaw, warm blue eyes, his shoulders too narrow for his height. Suddenly, she moved forward and dropped her bundle of belongings square at Tackett's feet.

"This is good place," she said to Joe. "This is better than my village." Her eyes went back admiringly to Tackett. "This is good place," she repeated. "I will stay here, please."

Tackett jumped back as if he'd been stung by a wasp. His face flushed scarlet. He glared down at the toes of his boots and edged away from the bundle Keetow had dropped before him.

Joe Meek slapped his thigh and shouted. Mr. Brandt laughed, too. Even little Debbie sent up a crow of laughter, seeing that laughter was in the air.

Keetow looked startled, and Ambrose, noticing this, said kindly, "Don't mind, we're not laughing at you."

She beamed. "Laughter is good. Among my own people, I remember, there is much joke and laughter."

"That's one thing you can't say for the missionaries," Joe Meek remarked. "They don't joke much, I bet, at the Mission where you came from; but they pray plenty."

"Prayer, too, is good," advised Keetow firmly.

"Tell her she can't stay here, Pa," Tackett muttered.

She flashed a glance, not admiring now. "I hear you well," she said in an icy voice.

"I caught Keetow sneakin' after me on the creek," Joe said. "I need advice how to handle her problem."

Joe pushed his hat back. He was fumbling for words when Deborah furnished a welcome interruption. She

had been staring, owl-eyed, at the strange girl in the brightly beaded dress. Now she rose and darted forward. Her hands clung to Keetow's fringed skirt; without words she begged to be taken up.

Tackett watched, amazed. Since they had come to Oregon, Debbie had made friends with no one. She wouldn't trust anybody but her father and himself; yet now she was begging this Indian girl to hold her. Since their mother had died, Debbie had not been in the arms of a woman.

"Wow," Tackett said. "She likes you."

"Yes," Keetow agreed matter-of-factly. Her hand

touched Debbie's hair. "Little yellow-head, you are very dirty. Come, I will wash you."

Tackett glared as Keetow carried the child toward the cabin. Dirty? Why, he had washed Debbie carefully just last night. It wasn't truthful to say the baby was dirty. That Indian girl was just trying to put him in the wrong.

"Who is she?" Ambrose asked in a low voice.

"One of the Mission young 'uns," Joe Meek explained. "A prize one, I reckon. She says they're bound to take her East, to show her off to the Missionary Board. But she's scared to go. Wanted me to help her get plumb away, to the Chinook village."

Keetow slowed her step, half-turned, her head cocked to listen.

"Are they planning to travel overland to the States?" Ambrose asked.

Joe Meek shook his head. "There's a missionary ship due this month. Mrs. Garret is figuring to board it."

Ambrose ran his fingers through his curly black beard and glanced toward the two figures making their slow way to the cabin. He had been wishing there was a way that he could send Deborah back to the States. This wild, lonely settlement was no place for a motherless little girl.

After their hard journey across the Rockies and the accident that had ended in his wife's death, Ambrose Brandt would never let Deborah go overland again. But if she could journey by ship . . . "I'd give a pretty penny for a chance like that to send Debbie East," he said.

At the cabin door, Keetow looked back over her shoulder in time to see Tackett's head jerk up defiantly. She saw the alarm spring up in the boy's eyes at the mention of sending this baby to the East. "Truly," she murmured, as she went into the cabin, "it must be a fearsome place."

Tackett swallowed hard. "Passage would cost a heap more than a penny, Pa!" he said.

Ambrose nodded, understanding his son's alarm. He knew that it would half-kill Tackett to have Debbie sent away. But it worried the father that she had no woman to care for her. It was in his mind that his own mother could give Debbie a real home and a woman's loving care. But his mother was far away, in Philadelphia. As Tackett said, ship passage cost a heap of money.

"I doubt if I could scrape up fifty cents," he sighed.

Joe Meek was still trying to study out the problem of Keetow. "What do you reckon we ought to do about that Indian girl, Ambrose?" He jerked a thumb toward the cabin. "She's plumb scared to go East."

Ambrose hesitated. "It would be a remarkable experience for her. And certainly she would not be happy now in a Chinook village. She has learned to live as white people do."

"You make sense," Joe agreed. "Likely 'twould be best to fetch her back to the Mission."

Tackett looked down at the bundle Keetow had dropped. He pushed it just a little aside and, with a sigh of relief, went back to lashing the poles on his fence.

Joe Meek took his knife from its sheath and began marking in the soft earth. "There's to be a settlers' meeting at Caleb Wilkins' place," he said softly. "Tuesday next."

Ambrose was poised to go to work again. He paused, frowning. "Another petition to Congress? Will it do any more good than the others have?"

The mountain man shrugged his shoulders. "We ain't figurin' on petitioning for Territorial Government this time."

"Just as well," Ambrose answered. "They might send us another Indian Agent."

Both men laughed. The only answers Congress had made to the petitions of the settlers had been to appoint Elijah White as agent to the Indians in this region. White had been to Oregon earlier as a missionary. When he had returned with his appointment, he had acted as though he were a governor. The settlers had demanded his authority. When he could produce none, they had laughed him out of office. How could they have a governor without a government?

Ambrose leaned against the fence and prepared to give his full attention to Joe Meek. Joe launched at once into talk about the meeting. He was full of it, and presently the two men walked off toward the woods, leaving Tackett to finish lashing the willow poles.

The boy was glad to see Joe Meek filling his father's mind with settlers' problems. He hoped there would be no room left for that crazy idea of sending Debbie away.

It wasn't as if he hadn't taken good care of his little sister—even if that Indian girl had stepped in, saying Debbie was dirty. Of course she had a little mud on her hands and face from playing on the ground—a body couldn't be watching every minute while fencing in a cow!

CHAPTER 2

Joe Meek Palavers

A cow was a mighty valuable animal in Oregon. Even a rangy longhorn like this, Tackett figured, was worth 5,000 split fence rails. Besides, if he could keep her and could tame her enough, the cow would provide milk for Debbie.

That had been the first thought in Tackett's mind when he caught sight of the creature ambling down to the creek to drink. He chuckled at the memory as he worked away, closing the last holes in the fence. It had been a fierce, hard struggle to rope her and keep her tied until the corral could be built.

A girl couldn't have done that, he thought, with a glance toward the cabin. That Indian girl could not rope a cow that would give buckets of foamy milk for his little sister!

Then a noise from the woods put the worrying thought of Keetow out of mind. Someone was approaching the clearing. It was not his father or Joe Meek. The swish and crackle of twigs, the sound of footsteps, came from a direction directly opposite to that the men had taken. Tackett put down his hammer and waited.

In a moment, the red-capped stocky figure of their neighbor, Louis Palette, came into view across the clearing. The little French-Canadian came swaggering straight toward the corral with a pleased smile on his face and a glint in his eye.

But Tackett saw the looped rope of braided bear-grass in Louis Palette's hand. He knew at once that he was due for an argument. He wasn't going to let that cow go to the first person who claimed her, no matter what his father said.

Louis Palette moved forward with an amiable grin. "Long time I don't see that crazy cow of mine," he beamed. "Two years now she hide in the woods! She got pretty nice calf, you think?"

Tackett scowled. "The calf's all right," he admitted. "But what makes you think this is your cow? I guess you had a brand on your animals?"

Louis shrugged. "Everybody knows she's mine. I see notice Mr. Brandt put up at Trading House. Now I come get her."

"This longhorn's a mean old bag of bones, Mr. Palette." Tackett tried to sound offhand. "Maybe she's not the cow you lost."

The little man snorted and said *his* cow was mean. All of the Spanish cattle the settlers had driven up from California five years ago were mean, troublesome creatures. But of course the Americans hadn't been satisfied to borrow good cows from the Hudson's Bay Company. They had insisted on bringing in their own stock. This is what they got—animals wilder than deer, meaner than bobcats.

"Why do you want her then?" asked Tackett hopefully when Louis Palette had run out of words. "Why don't you get one of the Company cows? Dr. McLoughlin will let you French-Canadians have anything you want."

"I like to *own* my cow," Louis muttered.

So the Company didn't even sell stock to its own "voyageurs" when they retired and took up farming, Tackett thought. That must be one of the ways the Hudson's Bay Company had of keeping Canadian settlers under its thumb.

Louis coiled his bear-grass rope smoothly. "I will catch cow now," he said.

Tackett looked toward the grove of trees that hid Joe

Meek and his father. "Maybe I ought to call Pa to help you," he suggested, trying to gain time. "That cow hasn't let anybody in the corral since she had her calf."

The ex-voyageur laughed and unfastened the gate. He had no fear of a cow. Had he not served Hudson's Bay Company for twenty dangerous years before he retired to his Willamette Valley farm? "So, little one," he murmured, encouraging the beast, as he swung the loop of rope carelessly. "If you will but lift the head one moment!"

The cow lowered her horns and nudged her calf aside. Tackett warned, "She did that just before she sent me a-winding yesterday."

"It is nothing." Louis shrugged.

He stepped closer, enlarging the loop. The longhorn bellowed loudly; her tail straightened behind her like a bar. Suddenly she charged.

Louis Palette came tumbling through the gate much faster than he'd gone in. The cow bellowed and circled the corral until she was with her calf again. Louis picked himself up, red-faced and rueful. "Firs' time I think she mine. Now I make for sure. That cow is meanest one I ever see."

The little Canadian stood undecided, his red cap over one ear, his coat covered with mud. "I give her minute to think it over." He looked around the clearing and remarked that he didn't see the baby. "That little one, she make plenty trouble for you," he said.

"No trouble," Tackett answered shortly.

"Sure," Louis argued. "You got big worry all the time. Why your papa not give her to my Marie?"

Tackett shook his head defiantly. Marie was Louis' Indian wife, with five children of her own and two boys she had adopted from her tribe. Marie and Louis had a big enough family, without begging for Debbie, too.

"I'll just keep on taking care of Debbie," the boy said. "You can't walk up and claim her, like you do the cow."

Reminded of his errand, Louis turned his attention to the longhorn again. He took a stand at the corral gate, studying the beast with narrowed eyes. He was just about to swing his looped rope when Ambrose and Joe Meek came out of the woods.

Seeing Louis, Ambrose hurried his step. "What's wrong, son?" he asked.

"He's trying to take my cow."

"Does she belong to Louis Palette?"

"He says so," Tackett admitted.

Louis moved determinedly inside the corral, ignoring the men. He hesitated as the longhorn lowered her head and straightened her tail. Then he suddenly spun about, dashed outside the gate, and slammed it behind him. He scratched his head. "I think maybe I shoot her," he grinned.

Ambrose's gray eyes darkened. "Then the calf would die," he said quietly. "Are you sure she's yours, Louis?"

Louis was certain. For two years he had thought that wolves had got her, but the moment he saw her, he recognized that trouble-making red cow.

"But the longhorns all look alike!" exploded Tackett. "You can't prove she's yours without a brand, and I think I've got more claim on her than you have because I found her running wild."

"You want to be thief, eh?" asked Louis, no longer amiable.

Tackett's face flushed. "Look out what names you call!"

Ambrose put up a hand. "The cow isn't worth hard feelings between neighbors. We've got no law here to decide this, so we must take your word, Louis, that the animal belongs to you."

Excitedly the French-Canadian cried, "Company agent will say if she is yours or mine. Always agent decide such matter for us. Come, we will go to Champoeg!"

"You know who'll get the cow if Hudson's Bay has the say about it," said Tackett. "And it won't be an American."

Louis swaggered like an angry rooster. He had tried to be patient with these Americans who were moving into the valley. They were seeking homes and farms, just as he and his friends did when they retired from voyaging. But the Americans wouldn't settle peaceably. Immediately they took claims; they started quarreling about government, separate from Company rule; they shouted for laws, for the right to decide all sorts of matters that had always been left in the strong British hands of Dr. McLoughlin at Vancouver.

Louis had often wondered why Dr. McLoughlin let these settlers come into Oregon country at all. As chief factor for the Hudson's Bay Company, he had a say about who could settle here and who could not. First, he had let the missionaries get a foot in Oregon's door. After the missionaries came a trickle of settlers—and mountain men—until now, there were a hundred or more Americans in the valley.

It seemed as if they brought nothing with them but trouble. Trouble they brought, and a copy of some bill which had been presented to their Congress promising them land. They claimed that the Linn Bill would guarantee each of them 640 acres, one square mile of land, half again as much for a wife, a quarter as much for each child.

Of course, Louis knew that the far-away American Congress couldn't guarantee anything to people here. This was Hudson's Bay Company land, and Dr. McLoughlin was the highest authority. Why couldn't these newcomers accept that authority?

They asked the Company for tools, for wheat seed, for help of every kind. They depended on the Company for all they needed to begin farming. Why couldn't they depend on it for government, too? Why must they hold these settlers' meetings, protesting this or that? Why must they send petitions to their Congress, asking for Territorial Government, for the right to make laws?

Why wasn't the British flag good enough for them? And why wouldn't they believe that the cow was his?

"You think I try to get cow by big lie?" he shouted. "Nobody ever say such thing to Louis Palette before!"

"Didn't you call me a thief?" asked Tackett hotly.

"Be quiet, Tack," ordered Ambrose. "Louis, I did not intend to question your word. The cow is yours. Take her and welcome."

"But not the calf," said Tackett. "She was born on American land."

Joe Meek's voice rose. "By the great shaggy mountain, I'm with you! I'll back that medicine with knives, guns, or bare fists."

Louis Palette did not answer Tackett. He merely moved to the corral again, looping his bear-grass rope. The moment he touched the gate, the red cow lowered her horns and charged. Louis leaped hastily aside as the cow hit the green willow bars with a crash. But he attempted a swagger as he straightened his red cap and tightened the belt of his coat.

"When calf is big, I come shoot that scoundrel," he growled.

Tackett caught Ambrose's warning glance and swallowed the words that had come to his tongue. He stared after the little French-Canadian as he disappeared in the woods. The boy supposed he'd have to let the cow go—unless Louis would let him split rails to pay for her. Five thousand of them, and probably as many more for her calf—it would take him half the winter.

Joe Meek, too, stared after the red-capped figure. "Company man," he snorted. His dislike for Hudson's Bay Company and all it stood for was in his voice. He had no use for anyone connected with it. These lords of the Northwest were to blame for spoiling the beaver trade for fur trappers in the mountains. Because of them, his wild, adventurous life was gone.

The mighty company had fought all independent traders who entered the regions where it wished to operate. It built trading posts beside those of the independent companies. It set trappers on the choicest streams with orders to strip the beaver ponds. No one had enough money to stand against such power.

Joe Meek, like many other mountain trappers, had found himself without a job. Used to wilderness ways, and unwilling to take his Indian wife and family East, he had drifted to Oregon.

This western land was claimed by the United States. But the hated Hudson's Bay Company was here, too. More firmly even than in the Rockies, it ruled the Indians and the white settlers. Under a treaty signed by Britain and the United States in 1818, the Hudson's Bay Company had built a permanent post on the Columbia River at Vancouver. It had spaced posts on almost every stream; it had settled its retired voyageurs in the rich Willamette Valley. It allowed no business except its own. Only the missionary or the farmer might settle here undisturbed.

So Joe Meek had taken to farming. For the first time in his restless life, he plowed and planted seed. He was not happy as a farmer, but he joined wholeheartedly with the other American settlers who were urging Congress to set up government. This would prove the American claim to the territory before the grip of Hudson's Bay Company was too strong ever to be broken.

While the British company was settling itself more firmly into the land, Congress was doing nothing. Representatives in Washington pointed out that the boundary of Maine was already the subject of bitter dispute with England. That dispute must be settled first, they said. Why couldn't Congress see that Oregon, with none of its boundaries set, would all go to Britain if her people stayed here too long unchallenged? Why couldn't it see that if American settlers lived under the British flag too long, England could claim them, too?

These were questions that Joe Meek had heard discussed by thoughtful Americans ever since he had come to the Oregon country. He signed the petitions that asked Congress to give them the protection of Territorial Government. He attended every settlers' meeting and added his chips to the smoldering fire of discontent with Company rule.

Joe Meek was an impatient man, a man of action; Congress was making no effort in the settlers' behalf. He felt that it was time for them to do something for themselves.

"Company man," he repeated, staring in the direction of Louis Palette's farm. "Have you heard that they brought twenty families of Scots and French-Canadians down from the Red River settlement?"

"I did," Ambrose nodded. "Also, I heard that the families are none too happy about it. It seems they were promised houses, farm animals, and land among their kinsmen here in the valley. When they arrived, they got nothing at all, unless they agreed to settle north of the Columbia, away from us. McLoughlin has shut off supplies to all who signed the last petition to Congress," Ambrose added anxiously. "Tackett and I have no more than a half-dozen charges of powder between us. I'm afraid they're going to cut us off, too."

"They ain't let me have none for months. I been scrapin' by on what I could beg or borrow," Meek answered darkly. "I tell you, Ambrose, we've got to organize."

"How can we? We quarrel among ourselves. Some are as afraid of the missionaries ruling us as of Hudson's Bay. The French-Canadians attend our settlers' meetings and vote 'no' to every motion we make—"

"They won't be at this next meeting," Joe Meek reminded Ambrose. "Like I was telling you, this is to be a secret meeting." He glanced cautiously over his shoulder and leaned nearer, as if the land were full of spies. "How do you favor independent government, Ambrose? A Republic of Oregon?"

"Man, that's a crazy idea," Ambrose cried.

"Under the treaty, the Company set up an empire here. What's to stop us settin' up a republic? Looks like we can't have the American flag. We won't have the British. So let's have our own. That's what Texas did."

"But the Texans had to fight a war with Mexico. I doubt we could raise up half a hundred men to fight England. No, no, Meek! I could never favor such a move. Whatever we do must be done by vote, not by force."

Joe sighed, ruefully, "That seems to be the general opinion, Ambrose." He stood up and thrust his knife back into its sheath. "You be there at Wilkin's place come Tuesday and hear what the boys got to say. But don't forget, we ain't invitin' the French-Canadians."

"Well, I won't tell Louis Palette," Ambrose answered. "But unless we can get Canadian support, I don't understand how we can organize any government. What good is a law for me that my neighbor isn't committed to obey? The Canadians depend on the Company for laws; why should they obey ours?"

"Let's worry about gettin' the law, first," Joe grinned.

Tackett listened, a little impatiently, to the talk of the men about law and government. He was discouraged because his father hadn't put up any fight about the cow. Likely as not, law or no law, Louis Palette was going to get her.

The boy moved away toward the cabin and called over his shoulder, "I'm going to get my gun and fetch some meat for the supper pot. There's plenty of grouse in the woods."

Tackett went to the cabin for his musket. The Indian girl was combing Debbie's hair. Tackett usually had to hold the baby down to do that and shut his ears to her howls. But Keetow was having no such trouble. Debbie's hair stood out, soft and golden; her eyes looked blue as flowers in her shining, clean face.

Tackett reached down to get his musket without a word. Debbie always went hunting with him, but this time he wouldn't even ask her. Let her stay with the strange Indian girl if she enjoyed getting all prettied up so much.

But Debbie jerked away from Keetow and dashed to the corner for the little wooden gun Tackett had carved for her. She pulled out the buckskin bag of pebbles that was her shot pouch. Humming gaily, she trotted after Tackett through the door of the cabin and across the clearing.

The boy couldn't help grinning triumphantly. She still liked him best after all.

Keetow busied herself building a fire on the clay hearth. She raked the ashes aside to find coals, then put on chips and blew gently until the flame caught. When she carried the iron kettle to the creek for water, Ambrose noticed and came to carry it back to the cabin for her. He saw the fire blazing brightly and the hearth swept clean.

"You make your own welcome, Keetow," he smiled. "You have had good teaching at the Mission."

"It was good to learn," she said. "Except I did not like to read in the books."

"Did your parents take you to the Mission?"

"Three women of my village took me there. My mother and father died long ago." Keetow answered the man's questions willingly.

"Then you don't remember much about your home, do you?"

"It was near the great salt water and very beautiful."

"Maybe," Ambrose volunteered as he went out the door again. "And maybe not—it's a long time that you've lived away from your Indian village."

The girl stood in the doorway staring defiantly.

In the woods, Tackett's musket boomed with a solid, kettle-filling thump. Keetow heard the shot and thrust another stick of wood beneath the kettle, coaxing the water to a quicker boil. A smaller pot, holding boiled wheat, bubbled slowly at the edge of the coals; the bowls and spoons were set out on the table. There were no more chores to do until Tackett brought in the game.

She sat quietly on the split long bench, watching the fire and waiting. But her heart beat with quick, rebellious rhythm. Joe Meek had failed her. He meant to take her back to the Mission instead of helping her find her own village, and more and more she feared the journey to the land of the white people.

She had seen the alarm leap in the eyes of the boy when his father spoke of sending the little yellow-hair there with Mrs. Garret. Truly then, the East must hold great dangers. More than ever she was determined not to go.

CHAPTER 3

White-Headed Eagle

Tackett swung his ax with the steady, confident stroke that practice had given. He enjoyed the challenge of the wood against his swing. With each jarring stroke, the blade took its yellow bite from the heart of the young fir tree. But the ax head was loosening. In a moment he must stop and drive in a peg to tighten it.

His father, working nearby, made a different rhythm with his ax. He was limbing fallen trees, and the sound was short and sharp, not solid and deep. With all the noise, it was hard to understand how Debbie could sleep. But there she was, curled on a bed of soft branches, hugging the stick doll that Keetow had made for her that day two weeks ago.

The Indian girl's visit, Tackett had to admit, had turned out all right after all. That grouse she had stewed was the tastiest food he'd eaten in a long time. And for once he hadn't had to do the cleaning up after a meal.

But she did have a bossy way with her. She had argued with Joe Meek against going back to the Mission. Even as she had climbed into her blue-stained canoe, she had made it plain that she didn't intend to board that missionary ship to go East again. Bossy and stubborn as a mule, she was.

The ax head was looser. After about two more strokes, Tackett decided, he would stop cutting and drive in that peg. He'd have to move to the other side of the tree then anyway.

His thoughts went back to the day of Keetow's first visit. Killing those three grouse with one charge of powder had been a mighty blessed thing. Even Joe Meek had praised that, and Joe didn't praise anybody lightly. There would be good hunting during the winter, if only he could get enough powder. Maybe the Company would sell him some if he could earn the money to pay for it. After all, he hadn't signed the settlers' petition to Congress.

If only he could get a few days' work, he would try to buy shot and powder at the Company store. But Louis Palette wouldn't hire him. Louis was still mad because he hadn't got the red cow home and wouldn't even talk to Tackett about splitting rails to pay for her. He'd be madder than ever, Tackett grinned, if he knew that she'd gentled enough to give down a quart and a half of milk just last night.

The ax head flew loose. It was hurtling through the air before Tackett quite realized what was happening. He heard his father give a little grunting sigh. The boy whirled to see Ambrose's broad figure fold to an ungainly heap upon the ground. The ax head lay there by his father's hand, half buried in fir needles.

Tackett groaned. Why hadn't he taken time to set the ax head tight?

Shivering, he grasped his father's shoulder and tried to straighten the limp form, but the boy's arms seemed made of straw, weak with emptiness.

Ambrose stirred and groaned, and a wildness of relief roared through Tackett. "Pa!" he shouted. "I was scared crazy!"

Ambrose's gray eyes opened slowly. There was a whitish mark on his forehead, already turning purple, where the back of the ax had struck. A drop or two of blood oozed thickly.

Ambrose looked up at the boy's frightened face. He

struggled to sit up. "I'm all right," he muttered. "Stop fussing, will you?"

He pulled himself to a tree trunk and leaned against it, letting the waves of dizziness roll over him. What if he had not been able to stir, to sit up? What if he had lain there quiet, never to move again? What would Tackett have done? And Debbie?

Ambrose Brandt's blurred gaze moved from the white-faced boy to the baby asleep on the fir boughs. Tackett could look after himself if he were left alone. Strong and quick and willing, he could earn his keep. But the boy couldn't care for Debbie, too. The Mission boarding school was only for Indian children; she couldn't stay there. Some already overworked wife of a settler would have to make room for Debbie. She would grow up alone, among strangers.

Ambrose touched his forehead gingerly. This had been a timely warning, he believed. It drove him to make a decision he had avoided. He would have to send the baby home to his mother.

If Mrs. Garret could be persuaded to take the child in her care, he'd arrange for passage somehow. Maybe his mother could pay at the end of the voyage. If Mrs. Garret would take Debbie—as she was taking Keetow . . . It was good that Debbie had been drawn to the Indian girl.

"Pa!" cried Tackett. "Are you all right? You look so queer—"

Ambrose shook the dizziness from his head. He did not try to tell the boy what he was thinking. How could he explain that sometimes you had to give up what you valued most to keep it safe? "My head aches," he said. "But that's natural after such a blow. I'll just take Debbie and go up to the cabin. You get back to work."

Debbie woke, yawning but bright-eyed as a squirrel. Ambrose swayed a little as he picked her up, then steadied himself and lifted her to his shoulder. He couldn't bring himself to look at Tackett as he said, "Tomorrow I plan to go upriver to the Mission. I'll have Doc Bailey look me over. It's nothing to worry about."

Tackett groped miserably among the fir needles for the ax head. His father must be hurt badly, or he wouldn't go twenty miles to the Mission to see a doctor.

"Nothing to worry about!" Tackett whispered angrily to the October stillness. "If he wasn't hurt bad, he'd have told me off for my carelessness."

∽

On his way to the Mission to see Mrs. Garret, Ambrose stopped briefly at the trading post at Champoeg. Joe Meek was leaning against the log wall of the Hudson's Bay Company warehouse. Ambrose could see that he was enjoying himself. Joe liked to come to this little town set high on the banks of the Willamette River and annoy the Company people. Sometimes he trapped and brought in a pack of beaver skins. He knew they wouldn't trade with him, but he liked to show that he didn't have to heed their rules against trapping.

Today he was especially pleased. Dr. John McLoughlin, the chief factor of the Company, was in Champoeg. Joe hadn't seen him yet, but he was certain that McLoughlin would presently appear. Meanwhile, he was telling his choicest bear story to an eager circle of listeners.

"I didn't know she was a she-bear with cubs," he explained, "or I wouldn't have tackled her. She was standin' there, strippin' berries into her mouth, and I took my gun and jumped off my horse and went trottin' up to her, bold and brass. I was maybe twenty paces from the bear when she turned. I upped and fired. But the cap burst without firin' the charge. I ran for my horse with the bear directly behind me.

"The boys were yellin' and shoutin' when suddenly the whole bunch of horses, mine among 'em, ran for the hills. I was left afoot with the bear outrunnin' me."

Ambrose laughed to see the attention Joe's yarn was getting. But he didn't stop to hear the outcome of Joe's fight with the bear. He had more important things to worry about. With a wave of his hand, he moved away from the group of idlers, the Canadians, Indians, and a couple of Americans, hanging on the mountain man's words.

"I rammed my rifle crossways in the bear's mouth," Joe's voice boomed. "I set the trigger while she was spittin' it out. I fired again but hit the beast low, just enough to make her mad. The bear grabbed the rifle outen my hand and threw it. She reached for me with her jaws wide open. There wasn't nothin' between me and certain death."

Joe's glance went beyond the circle of listeners and rested upon a tall, white-haired man who had quietly joined them. Joe's mouth twisted a bit, his back firmer against the log wall of the storehouse.

"Howdy, Mr. McLoughlin," he said quietly.

Canadians snatched off their red caps; Americans edged nearer to each other. Here was the most powerful man in Oregon, the man many feared but all respected. Big-framed, taller even than Joe Meek, with a mane of white hair, he was called White-Headed Eagle by the Indians. McLoughlin had earned the name partly because of his shoulder-length drift of snowy hair, partly because of the awe in which he was held.

McLoughlin had grave, thoughtful eyes, but an impatient manner of speaking. He could not understand these American settlers who wanted powder and supplies from the Company warehouses, yet refused to respect his authority. Often he helped them against his better judgment. Sometimes, however, he wondered if he shouldn't send them away as the Company expected him to.

"Well, Mr. Meek, well!" he said. "Killing Indians again, I see."

"Bear, this time, Mr. McLoughlin," Joe grinned.

"Bear or Indians, this yarning is a fearful waste of time. How many acres of wheat did you sow this fall?"

Joe's grin faded. His eyes narrowed warningly, but his voice remained careless and soft.

"Well, now, I reckon I sowed a few," he said. "Near about as many acre, maybe, as you shipped fur packs. How many was that, Mr. McLoughlin?"

The factor brushed aside Joe's words with a wave of his hand. "Come, Mr. Meek. It was not my intention to ask accounting, of course. But I admire industry. I like to see you newcomers industrious."

Joe rubbed his smooth chin with pretended thoughtfulness. "Might be I could accommodate you there, sir. I was noticin' a couple beaver ponds upcountry that made me feel downright industrious."

McLoughlin drew a sharp breath. "The beaver belong to the Company. When will you understand that? Forget your bear-killing yarns, Mr. Meek, and your foolish political play. Farm, sir, farm and live well, as my Canadians do!"

The Company men gave him a cheer that drowned out any reply Joe might have made. McLoughlin's smile appeared again as he made a small bow. With stately tread he returned to join his Champoeg agent waiting for him at the door of the Trading House.

Joe scowled. McLoughlin had not made the forty-mile river journey from Fort Vancouver for nothing. Nor had he mentioned "political play" idly. Joe wished that Ambrose Brandt had waited. He would have valued Ambrose's guess about McLoughlin's intentions.

To an American standing beside him, Joe muttered, "I'll warrant he's heard of the secret meetin' at Caleb's. He's here to see if he can't spring our traps empty."

A look of alarm crossed the other's face. "What do you suppose he'll do?" the man asked gingerly.

"I wouldn't know," Joe answered. "But we ain't backin' down, no matter what he starts."

The settler shook his head uneasily. "My wheat is in the Company granary, waiting shipment to the Russians in Alaska. If he takes it in his mind to punish us by refusing to ship and sell our wheat, it would ruin me. I wonder if I ought to go to that meeting after all."

With one swift motion, Meek pushed away from the wall and collared the settler. His voice roared out over the crowd, over the river. "If you are lily-livered enough to pull out because you are scared to lose your market, you will be under the Company thumb so long as you live!"

"But, Joe!" murmured the settler. "What will I do with my wheat?"

"Better to let it rot in the fields," roared Joe grandly, "than to give up Oregon to British traders."

There was a shocked moment of silence in the little crowd, then one of the Canadians said a jeering word in French. Another, encouraged, called slyly, "That bear, when she bite you, she die, maybe?"

Joe loosened his grip on the American, patted the man's collar back in shape, and grinned. "She got powerful sick," he admitted. "Riled sufficient, Joe Meek can trade bites, even up, with a rattlesnake."

CHAPTER 4

A Fight in the Grove

As the crow flies, it was four miles from the Brandt homestead to the Heathwires' new grist mill on Youder Creek. The distance as Tackett could travel it, walking beside the pony loaded with Debbie and a sack of wheat, was considerably farther. When his father suggested the journey, he had pointed to a notch or opening in the hills and said, "Go directly for that until you sight the creek. The mill will be thereabouts."

Tackett wouldn't admit to Ambrose his dislike of going to Heathwire's mill. He had never truly explained that Webb Heathwire's fists had caused the black eye he had gotten in Willamette Falls. That fight had taken place when the Brandts were waiting to take up their claim. There, in the dusty road of the little settlement, Tackett had listened to Webb Heathwire's voice jeering, "Nursemaid. I said you wasn't no more'n a girl, and you ain't."

Tackett had started the fight, but Webb had whipped him properly.

Webb would be at his father's mill again, sure as anything. And Tackett had Debbie along. She perched on the back of the red-spotted Indian pony and gripped the ropes with which Tackett had lashed the sack of wheat. Her yellow curls blew in the morning breeze; her head bobbed to the pony's loose-limbed walk. This trip was an adventure for Debbie, and she glowed with happiness.

Tackett wished that it wasn't quite so plain that her coat was made from his old jacket. Most anybody, seeing it, would recognize that it was cut down and made over. Webb Heathwire would surely guess that in the Brandts' womanless household, Tackett had done the sewing.

The carpet of fallen leaves rustled under the pony's hooves and under Tackett's feet. Oak trees stood almost bare but for the clinging mistletoe which knotted itself in gray-green patches against the dark wood. In summer you couldn't glimpse the mistletoe. But now, with the trees bare, every grove was full of it.

This morning Tackett's father had notched "1st of November" on his stick calendar. Any day now the rains would begin, and then, according to the old-timers, the downpour would last until March. That would be a lot of rain, thought Tackett, but likely they would mind it less than the deep snows of the East.

Out of the grove, they crossed one of the many prairies, rolling and clear. A convoy of grouse burst from the brown grass clumps just ahead; a flight of pigeons winged swiftly overhead.

He pointed the birds out to Debbie. "If only I had powder to spare, I could fetch some down with my musket!"

The pony paused and picked his way through the rough grass. Tackett stopped to tighten the rope that held the wheat sacks. Ambrose had brought the wheat home when he came from the Mission. He had paid for the two sacks of grain by a day's work at his old trade of woodworking.

It had been a real worry to Tackett when his father had failed to come home that night. Suppose, he thought, that Dr. Bailey had found something wrong with him and had kept him at the Mission for more doctoring? As the night wore on, he thought of other things that might have happened, too. The skiff might have overturned in the Willamette. Fighting might have started between American settlers and Canadians. Peaceable as he was by nature, his father might have been forced to join in. That had been the first night Tackett had noticed the wolves howling.

With daylight his father had returned in safety. He had only stayed over to work. He said his head was all right and there wasn't anything to fret about. But he was fretting.

Tackett could tell that his father had something on his mind he hadn't told. He was gentler-spoken than usual, and sometimes Tackett caught him staring in a brooding kind of way, almost as if he felt sorry about something. And he had not scolded once about the carelessness with the ax.

"Pa meant my trip to the grist mill to be a treat," Tackett said to Debbie. "He thought I'd like a day off from work to take his grain to the mill while he went to the settlers' meeting. I would like it, too, if we were going anywhere else. But that Webb is sure to start something."

Tackett shifted his musket to his left hand and touched his belt knife uneasily. He could protect himself against wolves or bears with such weapons. But against a boy like Webb Heathwire, you had to depend on your fists. Webb was a heap bigger and older, but that made no difference.

If he had to take another licking, Tack hoped Debbie wouldn't see it. She thought he was plumb wonderful now, but if she saw him whipped, she might never think so again. But he couldn't leave her alone, either, while he went ahead and had it out with Webb.

Debbie reached her arms to him, asking to be put down. Tack saw that she had a little dried milk on her upper lip, and he dabbed at it awkwardly while he held her in the crook of his arm. "Looks like I'll never get caught up with washing you," he said. "But I'd rather take a licking from Webb every time I meet him than let somebody else have the care of you."

Debbie was on the pony's back again when they reached Youder Creek. This tumbling, fierce little stream was a good choice for a mill race, thought Tackett. But he could see no sign of the mill.

Upstream or down, he wondered, and stood a moment, debating. A faint drift of smoke showed against the sky downstream. Slowly he turned and headed toward it.

As they crossed a small natural clearing, he noticed two gray squirrels darting about a hazel thicket that edged one side. Tackett saw that they were gathering nuts, and he wondered if he might find enough, still clinging to the boughs, to fill his own pockets. He pushed into the thicket, leaving the pony standing in the clearing and his musket leaning against a log.

Most of the nuts had fallen among the leaves, but he found a dozen or so. He was stowing them in his pocket when he heard the pony give a startled snort. At the same instant, something came hurtling through the air past his head and crashed into the bushes just beyond him.

Whirling, he saw Webb Heathwire standing in the clearing, big and ugly and grinning, with another throwing rock in his hand.

"If it ain't the baby nurse," jeered Webb. "Invading our land and stealing our hazelnuts! Get out o' that patch afore I aim this rock straight to your head."

The palms of Tackett's hands were suddenly sticky. His knees felt stiff, and his size shrunk to nothing beside Webb's. But he put the deepest scowl he owned on his face as he got clear of the bushes. "I'll fight you if I've got to," he said. "But I won't stand for stone-throwing. My sister might get hit."

"Wouldn't that be just too bad now?" jeered Webb. He tossed the stone in the air and caught it. "I wasn't figurin' on havin' to lick you again. My knuckles hurt for near ten minutes after last time when I loosed your tooth."

"You never did loosen it!" cried Tackett. "You never will."

"Any time I take a mind to, I can. Iffen Pa hadn't told me I oughtn't fight with them littler'n me, I'd do it now. 'Specially he wouldn't want me fightin' with a little old nursemaid." He looked at his rock. "Pa never said I shouldn't throw rocks wherever I want."

Debbie, who had been staring at Webb with round, wondering eyes, suddenly began to cry.

The blood roared in Tackett's ears. He took two blundering steps forward; Webb's face looked bigger and uglier. Webb was grinning as if he had been waiting for just that, for Tackett to begin. Maybe it would be better to take the jeers rather than tackle Webb and get beaten. The big boy might hurt him this time so badly he couldn't watch after Debbie.

Tackett was trembling as he turned to her. "It's all right, Debbie," he called. "There's nothing to be scared of."

Webb let fly the rock. It struck the pony just below the eye. The animal reared and lurched, and Debbie went tumbling. She hit the earth with a solid thump. Her cries ceased, and she was still.

"Guess that silenced her," said Webb in a half-scared voice.

Tackett didn't remember going for him. Afterwards, it seemed as if he must have dived through the air across the ten feet of space that separated him from Webb. He plowed into Webb, chest high. They sprawled to the ground together. Tackett's fists were going like hammers, but he was too furious to see where they struck. Webb hoisted himself from the ground and threw Tackett over his head and leaped on him.

Tackett's feet came up, and he rammed Webb back, then scrambled up and plowed into him again. When they hit the ground, they were like two wild animals, rolling, striking, gouging.

Tackett's jaw had a shattered feeling; there was pain like fire across his cheek. His only thought was that he had to end this fight in a hurry so he could see how badly Debbie was hurt. A dizzying curtain of black moved before his eyes. He rolled over, Webb's right arm clutched in his grip.

Suddenly Webb screamed. "Let go! Let go! You're bustin' my arm!" he groaned.

A fierce rush seized Tackett. He blinked to clear his vision and saw that he held Webb's arm in an unnatural position against the back of the boy's neck. He shoved the arm an inch higher, and Webb bellowed again.

It was a grand sound to Tackett's ears. "You give?" he demanded, scarcely daring to believe.

"Give," said Webb through a groan.

Tackett hesitated, then asked, "Will you be modest and polite and respectful to me and Debbie every time you see us? Say, 'yes, sir.'"

There was silence, and Tackett gave the arm a small shove. "Yes, sir! Yes, sir!" Webb's voice was rueful.

Tackett's happiness was complete when he looked over and saw Debbie scrambling to her feet, rubbing her eyes. The pony was across the clearing, headed for home in a steady, determined way.

Slowly Tackett loosed his grip on Webb. He wasn't sure he would find such a hold again. If Webb, freed, decided to start fighting again, the next round might have a different ending.

But the older boy had had enough. He stood, head down, shamefaced. "Don't tell Pa you beat me," he muttered.

"Catch the pony and bring her back here, and I'll never tell," said Tackett in a lordly voice.

It was good to sink down onto the fallen log while Webb, rubbing his arm, blundered off after the pony. Every bone in Tackett's body seemed to be aching, and he was afraid to move his jaw very much. There was a trickle of blood where a piece of skin was gouged from his thigh. But he kept his head high.

Without another word to Webb, Tackett hoisted Debbie to the pony's back and started toward the mill. The first drops of November rain began to fall, but neither rain nor anything else could dampen his joy.

The rain had steadied to a downpour when Ambrose reached Caleb Wilkins' cabin where the settlers were meeting to discuss the problem of government. He stamped mud from his boots on the log foot-scraper at the door and shook water from his ancient beaver hat. Then he called a greeting to the men gathered before the roaring fire.

Looking over the group, Ambrose thought one could scarcely believe that the seeds of government were here in the hands of the mountain men, missionaries, and plain farmer-settlers like himself. The newest arrivals in Oregon were the best-dressed, for they were still wearing the garments they had brought with them. Once those were gone, there was almost no way to replace them.

Some cloth was on the Trading House shelves, but it was designed for the Indian trade. A small amount of wool could be had from the Company, but there were no spinning wheels. It was patch and make do in Oregon. Buckskin and broadcloth alike were soiled and tattered, and blessed was the man who had a whole suit of either.

Ambrose noticed that Joe Meek had on his white satin waistcoat. It was his proudest possession. He wore it on grand occasions, buttoned over his buckskin hunting shirt.

But a man didn't brood about his clothes any more than he fretted about the rain. Good clothes and money in the pocket would come in time, and the rain would help bring them. Rain made the wheat grow. Thirty-three thousand bushels of wheat and 10,000 bushels of other grain had been harvested last year, shipped, and sold to the Russians in Alaska.

If a homesteader could scratch along for a year or two until he got a harvest, he could count most of his troubles over. He had credit at Hudson's Bay Company stores then. He had fields that would take the seed, shelled free in the last harvesting, and grow another crop without plowing or planting. He had time to worry about government—government and the Hudson's Bay Company.

An American citizen was used to feeling close to his government. He felt that it was designed for him, that he was important under it as men were nowhere else on earth. Transplanted to a part of the country where government did not operate, he felt lost and unprotected.

After he had provided himself with food and shelter, his next great concern was government.

In the States, this calendar year of 1842, citizens argued about slavery, about the Maine border, and about the annexation of the Republic of Texas. William Harrison, elected president, had served one month in office and died. He had been succeeded by John Tyler.

Slavery, annexation of Texas, and the very name of the president seemed far away and unimportant to the people in Oregon. In turn, the distant frontiersmen were largely ignored by the Easterners. No one in Washington gave much heed to the great raw country on the Northwest frontier, nor to the handful of Americans who had settled there. Congress was having trouble enough with England over the Maine border without quarreling over Oregon, too.

But the Americans in Oregon refused to be ignored, just as they had refused to live under English rule. Their fathers and grandfathers had fought in the wars against Great Britain. They had brought the memory of the Revolution across the mountains. They had no more love for England than had the men back in the States. Why, they asked, should Oregon be left to the British? It belonged by treaty to the United States. Why should the Hudson's Bay Company rule here unchallenged?

"The Company men have been here too long anyway," a red-bearded mountain man grumbled. "Think of the beaver they've took out of this country—and are still taking."

Ambrose edged to the fire, nodding and smiling at this one or that one that he knew. His curly black beard dripped water, and his boots oozed rain water with each step. The big room was hot and steamy with drying garments.

Joe Meek, near the door, watched the river with a wary eye. "Can't figure it," he muttered. "I was plumb sure McLoughlin aimed to throw a spoke in our wheels."

The meeting had not yet been called to order. Voices rose high as one man or another tried to be heard above his neighbor. Troubles were being aired and fears brought out in the open. These men were considering a move they knew was dangerous. They were recounting their reasons why they believed they were warranted in organizing themselves as an independent government.

"Hundreds of thousands of American dollars are going to England," said a tight-lipped man whom Ambrose recognized as William Gray. Gray had once been a missionary; he was now a claimholder. "But even that wouldn't be so bad if they would but leave us in peace. I know they are setting the Indians against us. I know it!"

"I cannot believe Dr. McLoughlin would do such a thing," cried Jason Lee.

"My faith in human nature is not so great as yours, Reverend Lee," returned Gray stubbornly. "The Hudson's Bay policy is, and has always been, to oppose any permanent settlement within their empire or on their trapping grounds. If they set the Indians against us, we could be destroyed in a night and nothing ever proved against the Company."

A red-faced little farmer knocked his pipe against the hearth. "I ain't worried about the Indians. It's kicking the bushel that I don't like. Hudson's Bay folk at the granary use their own wheat measure, bigger than our half-bushel. Then they kick it so it measures even more. And it's no use complaining. It's sell to them or don't sell at all. There's no law, nobody to make them treat us fair."

Joe Meek scanned the river. "Get to the business," he urged. "I smell trouble even if I can't see it."

But scarcely anyone heard him. Land rights were being argued now. "McLoughlin claims the whole town site at Willamette Falls," cried one man excitedly, "and the best water-power site on the whole river. He has kept the best town site and power site in the whole of Oregon for the Company."

"Why worry about one town site?" someone else asked. "Aren't they claiming the entire country?"

"But I've built my cabin there—now he says I've got to pay him for my claim or get off."

Robert Shortess moved behind a table and rapped with a stick for attention. "Gentlemen, I am calling the meeting to order. How many are here? Twenty-four? And everyone with a good reason for wanting government. Our question today is how to go about getting it.

"We have got to figure how we can set up an authority that will have laws and power to right our wrongs, settle disputes over land claims, punish crime, and defend our homes."

"I move it be put to the vote!" Joe Meek shouted. "Who's for the Republic of Oregon?"

Ambrose spoke up firmly. "I, for one, am not. Not only would we be defying Hudson's Bay Company, but the Congress of the United States. I am confident that in time Congress will extend Territorial Government to Oregon. I believe that we should wait."

Jason Lee nodded. "I am in agreement with Mr. Brandt. Congress will act for us in due time."

"We could wait forever," someone shouted.

Alanson Beers, also of the Mission, jumped to his feet. "It's my belief that Congress doesn't want to tackle the problem. It has been said, right in the Senate, that we are so far away we couldn't be protected. They say that a Territorial Representative would spend so much time traveling he would have only two weeks a year to speak for us in Washington.

"They figure that it would cost the government $3,720 every year just for travel between Oregon and the capital at Washington. No, they don't want to bother with us. If we are to have government, we must launch our own."

"Twenty-four of us against the world?" asked Ambrose. "With little power, no supplies, and not even a law book among us?"

As if a shot had been fired over a pond of ducks, a clatter of voices rose in protest, in agreement, in scorn. The chairman beat his stick against the log wall. "Silence, please. Silence!" he cried. "The meeting is in order. We will hear each man in turn."

For a moment, only the crackle of the fire was heard. In the quiet, a faint sound of singing drifted into the room. Joe Meek whirled to the open door, looked to the river, and groaned. "Hudson's Bay canoes!" he shouted. "A whole brigade of 'em, filled with Canadians. Three canoes, nine men to each. We'll make no government today, boys—they've got us outnumbered."

CHAPTER 5
A Ship is Here

Keetow crouched under the drooping wet boughs of a giant fir tree, watching the cabin door with a mixture of doubt and eagerness. If Mr. Brandt did not leave the cabin soon, she must go on, without offering the gift she had brought here. It would not matter if the boy saw her or the baby. They would not try to send her back to the Mission. But this time she would trust no grown white person to help her on the way to her village.

Last night, after she had left the Mission, she had stayed in the lodge of a family of the Tualitin tribe. They were very poor people: a father, mother, a sickly four-year-old boy, and a tiny baby strapped to a board. Their home had been crowded and smoke-filled. But she had been welcomed without question and invited to share their dried fish and the baked lily root called camas.

They had told her of an old trail that led over the hills to the Columbia River. Down the Columbia, they said, she would find the Chinook village.

She must abandon her canoe if she went by way of the Tuality trail. But even so, it would be better. If she traveled by canoe, she could not avoid passing the white settlement and the branch of the Mission at Willamette Falls.

Keetow pulled her blanket tighter around her. Her heart stirred uncomfortably as she thought of Mrs. Garret. That day when Joe Meek took her back to school, the missionary had cried and put her arms around Keetow. She had called Keetow "daughter."

"I was worried," Mrs. Garret said. "My little daughter, why did you run away?"

Mrs. Garret had talked much then of the white people's country and how peaceful and pleasant it was. Keetow did not think that Mrs. Garret could lie, but she did not understand how it was that so many left a land such as was described. They traveled far, far, by dangerous ship or trail to come here to transplant themselves in the Siwash country. Would they do that if their own land was good?

The cabin door was opening. The boy, Tackett, stepped outside with an ax in his hand and went to the lean-to where the firewood was piled. The door stayed open behind him, and Keetow could see inside the cabin, cozy and bright with the glow of the fire. The little yellow-haired one was there, but Keetow could not see the father. It might be that he was still asleep.

As the boy stood up with wood in his arms, Keetow moved from her hiding place among the trees, calling softly. He turned, startled. "Oh, it's you!" he said. "Running away again, I expect."

She made a sign for quiet. "I did not want your father to see me," she whispered.

"He won't. Pa is down at the Falls making some cupboards in the new Mission house. He'll be gone a couple more days, I expect."

He watched in silence as she went ahead of him into the cabin. If she wanted to, she could cook breakfast, but she wasn't to get the idea he was glad she'd stopped to see them.

Debbie gave a cry of pleasure at sight of the Indian girl. Tackett's jaw set as he saw her arms around the neck of the visitor. He didn't see why Debbie thought this girl was so wonderful.

Keetow laid aside her blanket and opened her bundle of belongings. She had a little dried fish and corn for her journey, her good dress of beaded doeskin, her comb, soap, and a flint and steel for making fires. From underneath all these, she drew forth the moccasins she had made for Debbie.

The little girl's leather shoes had long been outgrown and discarded. Ambrose had replaced them with moccasins bought from the merchant Indians at the Dalles, but these had always been stiff and uncomfortable.

"Made of green buckskin," Keetow said scornfully as she cast them aside. "Siwash do not make such kind for himself." She slipped the small, soft new moccasins on Debbie's feet. "These I made of lodge skin, cured by smoke and rain and sun. These will never be hard or slippery."

Tackett looked at his own shoes where he'd cut out the leather to make more room for growing. "I wouldn't mind a pair like that for myself," he said.

Keetow slowly wrapped her belongings again and took up her blanket. Tackett said cautiously, "We haven't had breakfast yet. If you're hungry you can stay."

She hesitated. "I have far to go and small time. I wish to be with my own people before the great ship of the Mission reaches the Falls."

"Is it in the river?" Tackett asked eagerly. He had never seen a sailing ship, having been born on the inland prairie country. There would be great excitement when it anchored below the Falls. There would be mail aboard it, papers, news from the East, missionaries, and maybe some settlers. "I just wish I could be there to see it."

"But you will see it," said Keetow, surprised. "When the little yellow-hair goes to the ship with Mrs. Garret, will you not be there to say goodbye?"

For a minute the sense of Keetow's words wasn't clear to Tackett. "What are you talking about?" he gasped. "Debbie isn't going on the ship!"

Keetow studied his face thoughtfully. Surely the voyage

to the land of the white people would be filled with many dangers and terrors, and the home they had abandoned must be a terrible place. The boy was brave, yet he was badly frightened at the thought of his sister going.

"Your father asked that Mrs. Garret take the little one with her," she explained gently. "There was water in his eyes like the tears of a woman when he asked it."

"But he couldn't get passage for Debbie!" cried Tackett. "He hasn't got enough money."

"I do not know of that, but I think it is true that she will go."

Tackett knew that it was true. That was why his father had acted so uneasy lately. He'd looked at Tackett as if he felt sorry for him. His father had started, half a dozen times, to say something, then stopped as if he couldn't find the words.

The boy's jaw set hard. The knuckles on his hands were white; his nails pressed into his palms. "I'm going out to tend the stock," he blurted. "Watch Debbie a minute until I get back."

He strode outside, filled with a wild rebellion. His father had no right to do that. No right! Debbie was his, Tackett's. He loved her more than anybody else did.

He had been studying in the Blue Back Speller and reading some out of the Bible book every night so he wouldn't forget his own learning. He had to be smart enough to teach Debbie when she was ready. He had been making a little house for her doll for Christmas.

He stumbled blindly to the corral. Then he stopped short. The gate was broken down. The cow and her calf were gone. Tackett stood staring at the trampled mud, not seeing what it meant. His mind was a turmoil of unhappy thoughts of Debbie; of anger at his father; of the long, lonely winter ahead.

Slowly he realized that the animals were gone. Had Louis Palette taken them? No. There was the story in the mud, the doglike marks that circled the corral. Wolves! The wolves had come down from the hills after the cow.

But the red cow must have held them off. She was a match for wolves no hungrier than these in November. She had broken free and made a run for it with her calf. He found the torn, stripped carcass of one wolf. Tracks of the pack overlay the hoof marks of the cow and calf, headed for the grove.

Tackett's fury was partly aimed at the wolves, partly at the news he had heard from Keetow. At a dead run, he went back to the cabin for his gun. He could kill wolves, even if he couldn't stop Debbie from going away from him.

As he took down his musket, Debbie hurried to find her little gun. "No, you can't go this time," he said. "You stay with Keetow." He was shaking with misery and anger as he pushed her toward the Indian girl. "I ought to run away with you, like Keetow's doing," he groaned. "Only we haven't got any tribe to go to."

⁓

The best part of the day was gone when Tackett plowed his way back to the cabin. He had neither wolf skin nor red cow to show for his efforts. He had lost the trail in the wet woods, but stumbled on, hour after hour, until the wild misery in him settled to a dull, quiet ache.

It was strange, though, to see no curl of smoke from the cabin chimney. Keetow didn't seem like one who would carelessly let the fire go down. As he pushed open the cabin door and saw the empty room, he thought they were hiding from him and called resentfully. This was no time for jokes.

But they weren't hiding. They weren't in or near the cabin. He shouted through the rain, but only the pony appeared.

There were muddy tracks on the hard-packed, earthen floor of the cabin. He hadn't noticed these at first, but now he saw them, some overlaid by his own footprints. He felt an icy terror as he studied the mark of the big, clumsy shoe. A man or a big boy had been in the cabin.

Memory stirred as he noted the rough line across one sole. Webb Heathwire's boots had been patched with a square of leather over the toe, folded over and nailed down. Webb's boot could leave a tread such as this.

Outside he found more of the prints, some coming toward the cabin, some going away toward Youder Creek again. Were they heavier going away? He could not be sure. The pony had trampled the mud, and his own feet had blurred the tracks, too. But here were moccasin prints—Keetow's, he thought, for they were too large to be Debbie's.

Suddenly he was sure he knew what had happened. Webb had come here trouble-hunting. Keetow had seen him, and, fearing to be discovered and sent back to the Mission, had slipped away.

Webb had taken Debbie just to scare Tackett. Webb wouldn't dare hurt Debbie, Tackett told himself over and over. Likely he was standing over there just inside the woods, holding his hand over her mouth so she wouldn't call.

But neither Debbie nor her captor were hiding in the grove.

Swiftly Tackett tossed a rope and a blanket saddle on the pony and flung himself astride. Webb's trail led to the creek ford, and Tackett pushed the pony across and found more footprints on the other side. Webb had skirted the wheat fields; he was staying on the open prairie, not headed for the woods after all. Could it be that he was going home? That he was taking Debbie all that way? Tackett kicked the pony to a clumsy gallop.

At the far side of the wheat field, a splash of red through the gray of the rain caught his eyes. The red cow! And there, beside her, was the calf. She had come home. But finding the cow no longer seemed important.

Like a whirlwind, the little pony went driving up to the grist mill. Tackett yelled and shouted as if he were bringing an Indian alarm.

Webb was leaning against the mill door. His mouth dropped open, and his eyes blinked as he saw that the rider was only Tackett Brandt. But Tackett was wilder acting than he'd been that day by the hazel thicket.

"I was just over to your house," Webb began.

"Where's my sister?" howled Tackett. "What did you do with her?"

"I never saw her, Tack. I come over to ask would you accommodate me by showing me that wrestling hold. I been trying to figure it out on my big brother, and it wasn't no ways like you—"

"You hid Debbie! You're just trying to get back at me! I tell you, Webb, I'll bust both your arms if you don't tell me where she is."

"Honest, Tack," Webb's eyes clouded. "I never saw her! Nobody was in your cabin when I got there." Webb's big ugly face showed concern. "I just came over to your house to see would you show me that wrestling hold," he repeated.

Tackett realized that Webb was telling the truth. "That Indian girl took her," he said. "I might have known it. I've wasted all this time."

He was on the pony and gone again before Webb could ask anything more. Puzzled, Webb turned toward the mill and saw Louis Palette, who was waiting to have his wheat ground.

"I guess there's real trouble," yelled Webb. "The Indians have stoled the Brandts' kid."

"No!" cried Louis. "This bad thing. Dr. McLoughlin will be very angry."

Webb's father came hurtling down the ladder. "Like fun he will," the man blurted. "More likely, McLoughlin sicked 'em on to it. Indian trouble! Webb, go fetch my rifle."

CHAPTER 6
"Indians Stole Your Baby"

The ship from the Atlantic coast had entered the bay of the Columbia; she was on her way upriver. Ambrose Brandt's heart went heavy as lead when he heard the news. He wished now that he had had the courage to tell Tackett sooner of the arrangements he had made for Debbie's passage. He wished that it did not seem so needful for the little girl to go.

Within ten days or two weeks, the vessel would sail again. They would bring Debbie here to the Falls, and they would say goodbye to her. For who knew how many years?

Even now, Mrs. Garret at the Mission was stitching the little dresses and cape she had offered to make for Debbie to wear on the journey. A good woman, a kind one, who had lost her husband here in Oregon and was giving up missionary work and going back East—it was she who had suggested that Ambrose build these cupboards at the new Mission. This gave him money to pay for the cloth used in Debbie's clothes.

Half the people from the settlement had taken canoes downriver this morning to meet the ship as it turned from the Columbia into the Willamette. In spite of the rain, they were making a holiday of the occasion.

But Ambrose stayed with his cupboard-making, and Joe Meek stayed to talk to him. Joe was as moody as Ambrose, but for a different reason.

"I can't but think how McLoughlin must be laughin' to himself," the mountain man said.

"We should have barred Caleb's door to the Canadians or tumbled them back in the river like I wanted."

With difficulty Ambrose turned his mind to the settlers' meeting that had been invaded so amiably by the Canadians. Smiling, bowing, they had crowded into Caleb Wilkins' cabin.

They, too, were concerned with government, they had announced. They had come to join the Americans with their advice and their votes on any matter that might be brought up. They knew, of course, that they would be welcome. Did not the Americans boast that it was their way to give every man his vote?

Stubbornly, Robert Shortess again had called the meeting to order. But it had soon become very clear that the Canadians would vote only "no" to every motion. The Canadians would not vote to appoint a committee to study the need for a governing body. They would not organize a committee unless it would disapprove a motion to organize a militia. They voted "no" on the appointment of a sheriff. They repeated their "no" to every motion.

Ruefully, the Americans began offering wild suggestions. Someone moved to widen the Willamette River. Someone else moved to build a road from the Falls to the Dalles on the Columbia.

"No! No!" howled the Canadians.

"I move to establish a circulating library!" chuckled a settler, making the most outlandish motion he could think of. The motion was seconded. The chairman laughed and called for a vote. He didn't suppose that anyone in the room possessed a book other than the Bible.

The Canadians looked around. They winked and nodded to one another. They would surprise the Americans. This time they voted "yes."

Joe Meek shook his head moodily, remembering. "It was a pretty job of out-generaling us," he remarked to Ambrose. "Not a word of trouble, but we get a circulating library instead of a government. The whole country's laughin' at us."

"We were going at this too hot-headed anyhow," Ambrose answered. "The only motion of any real value was the one for the appointment of a study committee. A committee could at least determine the form of government we might consider."

"One good thing came from the library talk," said Joe, brightening. "Somebody turned up a book that's got the law code of Iowa printed out. There's nothin' wrong with Iowa laws, accordin' to folks from that territory."

"A law code will be useful." Ambrose nodded. "It's surprising the number of books that have been put in the library already."

"I gave *Scottish Chiefs*," Joe confessed. "It's tattered, but reasonable yet. Even the French-Canadians gave some books, I hear tell."

"I believe they are really pleased with the idea, even though it was begun as a joke. One of them is reading my *Iliad* now." Ambrose groped for words. "It makes me wonder," he said. "If we could find other things beside politics to bring us together, I think the Canadians would go along."

Joe cocked an eyebrow. "Bait 'em, Ambrose? Get them in the habit of votin' 'yes', then drag them into government by the back door?"

Ambrose placed one of his precious nails at the place marked for it on the cupboard. With the hammer poised in his other hand, he glanced at Joe. "I was only thinking that they might understand our problems better if they shared a few of them. They are not concerned about crime, law, land claims, or markets. They leave all that to the Company."

"Bait's what we need," said Joe.

But he hadn't got beyond turning the idea over in his mind when a wild-haired, overgrown boy came shouting up the muddy path.

"Mr. Brandt! Mr. Brandt! Where be you, Mr. Brandt?"

"Here!" called Ambrose. "Right here, young fellow."

The boy plunged into the room. He stopped short and stared at Ambrose and at Joe Meek as if suddenly struck speechless.

"Well, sir, what can I do for you?" Ambrose asked.

"I'm Webb Heathwire, Mr. Brandt," the boy blurted. "Pa sent me to tell you—to tell you—" He swallowed hard. "Mr. Brandt, the Indians have stole your baby."

Tackett looked at the gray sky growing grayer and kicked the pony to greater speed. He tried to think clearly as they went rushing across the prairie. He had wasted so much precious time. Now it was near the close of day, and he hadn't even begun to look for Debbie.

Keetow would be traveling in her dugout canoe, but he couldn't follow her by water because his father had taken the skiff to the Falls. His mind raced like the pony's heels. Louis Palette owned a dugout! He could borrow that, whether Louis was willing or not. Tugging the bridle rope, he turned the pony to the left, toward Louis' place.

Louis wasn't home. Marie, his Indian wife, shook her head when Tackett asked for the canoe.

"I'm taking it anyway," Tackett yelled, and he ran to the landing.

He had already launched it and caught up the paddle when she came panting down to the creek, waving a long-bladed knife and shouting "Thief!" in two languages.

Hastily he pushed out into the current. "I'll bring it back," he called. "I'll bring it back as soon as I can."

"Wolf take the pig; American take the canoe!" she wailed.

She had forgotten to mention the cow, Tackett thought ruefully. Louis would have him in the Company prison, first thing he knew.

But his mind wouldn't stay on that worry long. The shadows of night were pushing down through the trees and the brush, crowding over the creek. Darkness would be on him before he even got to their own place. In half an hour it would be too black to see a length ahead of the canoe.

The light craft jumped through the water under his

hurried strokes, but even as he tried to send it faster, he knew that it was hopeless to attempt to follow Keetow and Debbie tonight. Waiting until morning would be hard, but better than hunting blindly in the darkness, to pass them, perhaps, or to split the dugout open on a rock or unseen log.

He tied up the dugout at his own landing. The cabin was cold and dark. He groped his way through the darkness, praying that he would find a live coal under the ashes. He crouched on his heels before the hearth until he saw a spot of glowing red, then fed the spark tenderly with twigs of pitchy wood. He tried not to think of Debbie, out in the night somewhere with the Indian girl.

The cow and calf had gone into the corral. There was some cheer in seeing that the longhorn now considered this her homeplace. She could roam freely now as the pony did. The calf could have all the milk tonight, too. No use milking when Debbie wasn't there.

The night passed slowly. Tackett hadn't expected to sleep, but he was more tired than he realized. Once he wakened with his heart hammering, thinking he heard Debbie crying. But it was only a wildcat screaming far away in the woods. The cry was like a child's.

At daybreak he cooked breakfast for himself and packed food, fire-making tools, a blanket, and his freshly sharpened knife. He debated about taking his musket. It was a heavy thing to carry and almost useless since he had but one charge of powder. But that one load might be important.

Just as the first light touched the sky above the Cascade Mountains, he was at the creek, where he had beached the borrowed canoe. A hundred yards below the cabin, beyond a sheltering clump of willows, he found Keetow's and Debbie's footprints where they had launched the blue-stained dugout.

The creek was higher today, swollen with rain, and muddy. Until the light improved, Tackett pushed the canoe cautiously. He was cool-headed this morning, knowing that his haste of yesterday had cost him the chance of finding Debbie easily. The curves and windings of the creek made the going slow, but when at last he shot into the broad Willamette current he made faster progress.

It was in his mind that Keetow would be avoiding people. Somewhere above, he thought, she would go ashore. But how would she go on from there? Light as the canoe was, she couldn't carry it far. Surely she wouldn't try to walk to the Chinook village. With Debbie!

He stayed close to shore as he went downriver. He wished Joe Meek were with him. He wished he knew more about the country. He had been in the Falls only twice. Of the country beyond the river's banks he knew almost nothing. Where would Keetow go ashore?

It was only by chance that Tack saw the blue canoe. The river had split to go around an island. He was turning into the inside passage when he glanced over and saw the blue prow nose into sight around the outer side of the island. With a thrust of the paddle, he changed course.

But as the canoe came wholly into view, he frowned uncertainly. A man, alone, was in the blue canoe. He was an Indian, who looked neither right nor left, but paddled intently against the force of the current.

Perhaps it wasn't Keetow's canoe. There could easily be others like hers, stained that color of the sky. But surely no other would have that long-legged little fawn poised just so on the prow. Tackett shouted again and dug in his paddle.

His uncertainty changed to anger. That was Keetow's canoe. And how had this man got it?

Plainly the Indian was trying to avoid him. He was a skilled boatman and could easily have outpaddled Tackett if the strong river current had not favored the boy.

"Stop, you!" Tackett yelled. "Where did you get that canoe?"

He was near enough to see the Indian's dark features, the braids of hair, the sloped forehead of a Chinook.

The Indian glared at Tackett silently, then bent to his paddling again.

Tackett headed straight for the blue canoe. "Hey!" he yelled. "If you don't stop, I'm going to ram you."

CHAPTER 7
Tackett Begins a Search

When news of Deborah Brandt's disappearance reached the great fort at Vancouver, Dr. McLoughlin called his swiftest Indian boatmen together. "Go to the Molalla," he said to one. "Go to the Callapooias," he said to another. He named a messenger to each tribe of the natives in the Willamette Valley.

"Tell them the American child must be returned," he said. "Tell them the anger of the White-Headed Eagle will be terrible toward her captors, toward any who harm her."

He sent word to a company of trappers which was making up at the farm opposite Wapato Island. This brigade, headed for the Umpqua trade in the southwest of the Oregon country, would not travel by canoe but by horseback, by way of the Tualiti trail. "Watch for the white girl," McLoughlin ordered. "Ask of every native you meet."

The Indians about the fort looked at one another uneasily, silently asking who had done this thing. No one knew. The trail of information that led from fort to settlement, from farm to Indian village, was usually as swift as burning gunpowder. For once it failed. No one knew who had stolen the American child.

Meanwhile, Joe Meek traveled upriver with Ambrose. "Don't fret," he said grimly. "We'll find that young 'un."

The cords of Ambrose's neck stood out like ropes as he pulled his oars against the current. "I suppose I shouldn't blame the Heathwire boy for delaying until today to tell me. But I can't understand Tackett leaving the baby alone yesterday. That's the part I can't understand at all."

Joe scowled silently. There should be half a hundred men organized to help with this hunt. But where were they? They had all hurried home to see that their own families were safe. There was no one to tell them what they must do, no authority to order them to organize. If this was the beginning of Indian trouble, it would be each man for himself. Joe shook his head and tried to set his ragged oar stroke to Ambrose's.

Louis Palette was waiting for them at the Brandt cabin. He had brought a horn of powder and a pig of lead. He gave what information he could, but he knew little more than Webb Heathwire had told, except that Tackett had borrowed his dugout.

"My Marie sorry she make a big fuss," he said.

Joe went like a rangy bloodhound sniffing and scanning the earth about the cabin clearing and along the creek. The heavy rain had wiped out marks of the dugout along the creek bank. But Joe pointed out where Webb had been, where Tackett followed him, where the wolves had gathered. He showed them the clean bones of the dead wolf.

"But I'm blessed if I see moccasin prints," Joe puzzled. "Only for these little ones, scarce longer than my hand. If an Indian's been here, he was a mighty little one."

A sudden thought made him look at Ambrose. Ambrose struck his fists together. "Keetow!" he exclaimed.

"Keetow. Gone to the Chinook village," Joe shouted.

"Taking my little girl with her."

Both men whirled on Louis. Exactly what had Tackett said? Louis spread his hands. He had seen the boy only as he galloped away. Webb had repeated his words—Indians had stolen the baby.

But Webb wasn't too bright. Maybe Tackett had said, "The Indian girl stole Debbie."

"That would fit," cried Ambrose. "I couldn't understand Tackett leaving Debbie alone, but he wouldn't have been worried at leaving her with Keetow. Keetow knew I planned to send Debbie East on the same ship with Mrs. Garret—it must have been in the girl's mind that she could save Debbie from the journey while she saved herself."

"Then they traveled by canoe," Joe nodded. "That's why Tack took Louis' dugout."

"But where did they go? Surely they would have been seen if they'd passed the Falls. Tackett would have stopped there to tell me if he followed them that way," Ambrose said.

It was Louis who remembered the Tuality trail. Indians and some of the Company men used this route to the Columbia, but few of the newcomers thought of overland travel here, where a stream led almost anywhere one wanted to go. The Tualatin River entered the Willamette about two miles above the Falls; up the Tualatin, perhaps ten miles, was the spot where the trail crossed the stream.

"Come, I will show you," cried Louis.

But somebody had to take word to the settlements that the Indian alarm had been a mistake. Joe swore he could find the trail without help, and Louis agreed to go to Champoeg and calm the settlers.

"Louis ain't a bad little voyageur even if he is a Company man," Joe said aloud as he and Ambrose once again took to the skiff. "This is the first time my powder horn weighed proper since I been in Oregon."

Ambrose felt almost lighthearted, so great was his relief. A night out in the cold and rain would have been uncomfortable for Debbie but likely would do her no harm. Perhaps, even now, Tackett had found her and Keetow. Perhaps at this moment he was bringing them back upriver. Then Mrs. Garret would take Debbie in charge and bring her safely to Philadelphia.

⁓

But Tackett was alone on the Tuality trail. Across the prairies it led, to rising ground and forest. Already the afternoon was well advanced; time, time was against him still.

The old Chinook had proved a stubborn fellow. He wouldn't say where he had got Keetow's canoe, or where the girls were. He refused to give any information at all until Tackett had raised his musket. Then he burst out in a jumble of words. From the jumbled talk Tackett could gather little information.

"Show me," said Tackett, and grimly pointed his gun until the man decided to understand.

With a long glare at the musket, he turned the blue canoe and headed back downstream. At the mouth of the Tualitin River, he would have stopped, but Tackett saw no

sign of the girls and urged him on. Up the winding river, on and on. At last they came to a wide place in the river, clearly a ford, for on either side was a faint trail.

The Chinook pointed north. He hit the prow of the blue canoe with his hand, he pointed to himself, repeated *salmon* loudly and made the sign for two, then pointed along the trail again. The meaning of that, as well as Tackett could tell, was that the Chinook Indian had traded salmon to two people for the canoe.

It made sense, Tackett decided. If Keetow had intended to travel by land, she would have to leave the canoe anyway and would have been glad to trade it for food she could carry. Frowning, he decided that he must believe the Indian.

It was as well that he did. Not far along the trail, he found the print of a small foot clearly marked in the soft earth. Debbie's! And a bit farther along, he found the place in a grove of firs where they had made camp for the night. Against the base of one tree was the little wooden gun he had carved for Debbie, looking forlorn there and forgotten.

But if they had camped here in the night, they were far ahead of him now. They would have started from camp in the morning, at almost the same time that he had left the cabin. Even allowing for the slowness of Debbie's travel, they would be far ahead along the trail.

He looked up at the sky and began running. He had to find them before another dark. He had to!

〜

"I'll make you another gun," Keetow said to Debbie impatiently. "As soon as we stop again tonight at a camping place, I'll make it."

She had said the same thing a dozen times since Debbie had first missed her forgotten treasure. The little gun must have been left behind at their camping place. But they had been following the trail for an hour before Debbie noticed that she no longer held it clutched in her hand.

Then the child had cried so bitterly that Keetow almost turned back to look for it. Good sense, however, had told her to keep on. She didn't want to spend more nights than needful on the trail.

Keetow had not expected the night to be so long and so frightening. "You must not be afraid of the night," she had said to Debbie. "Once, I was afraid of the darkness, but at the Mission I learned that the great God made the night so that we might rest from the work of the day. True, there are animals that roam the night, but we'll make a fire and that will frighten them away."

But making a fire had not been easy. Keetow had watched men at the Mission drop a spark from flint and steel onto tinder. She had seen how the spark would glow and catch and become a hungry flame.

The girl had been confident that she could get fire, for the rain had ceased, and she had found dry twigs and cones under fir needles. Again and again she had struck a spark. The spark had fallen to the tinder, glowed for an instant, and died.

"Surely there is fire here," she had said to Debbie, who stood watching uncertainly. "How did my people make fire in the days before white men came? When we reach my village, I will ask the old people. Old ones are wise."

Debbie had not looked very happy. There had been an anxious look in her round blue eyes as she gazed first at Keetow's face and then at the fire-making efforts.

Keetow had struck another spark, which glowed, faded, and seemed to die like the others. Then it came alive, a tiny flame. Debbie had crowed gaily and had thrust a cone into Keetow's hand.

"Indeed," thought Keetow as they trotted along the trail in the morning light, "fire is a very good thing."

She had cooked some of the dried salmon the old Chinook had given her and had made a very good supper. They had had more of the salmon for breakfast.

"It was very fortunate we met the old one from my village," she said. "At least we have food to eat on the journey. The Tuality trail is very long."

Keetow sighed as she spoke, remembering that she had lent her canoe to the Chinook in return for his precious food. She might never see her canoe again. Long ago, her people had brought her to Jason Lee's Mission in that blue-stained dugout with the fawn carved on its prow. How frightened she had been that day! How her heart had cried!

Mrs. Garret had been only a stranger, an enemy to bite and kick. When the Chinooks had gone away and left her, only the blue dugout had been comforting and familiar. But what a surprise it had been when Mrs. Garret had the canoe brought inside the Mission house so Keetow could spread her blanket in it to sleep. After that, she had never thought of Mrs. Garret as an enemy. She had two "loves" at the Mission: her canoe and Mrs. Garret, who called her "daughter."

Now she had given them both up. She had run away from Mrs. Garret, and she had traded her canoe for food. But that was necessary. She could not have carried the canoe along this trail, and she must travel the trail to get to her village.

Even now, while she was running away, she felt grief that she would not see her friend again. But perhaps she and Debbie could watch the ship carrying Mrs. Garret when it sailed past her village to the ocean.

Keetow remembered a place near the village where you could look far out over the water. When she was a child, not much older than Debbie, her mother had taken her to the old, abandoned fort, high above the water.

White people had built the fort on a point of land extending into the bay of the Columbia. She could remember clearly the broken, fallen walls of the fort. She could hear her mother's voice telling the story of the great ship that brought white people to build it.

"My grandfather was one of the chiefs of the Chinooks," she said, lifting Debbie in her arms to comfort her. Keetow talked steadily to the child as they made their way through the forest. It was plain that the sound of her voice was soothing to the little girl. It did not seem to matter if she spoke in English or in her own language.

"My grandfather was called Concomley, and he had but one eye, for the other had been blinded by the spear of an enemy. My grandfather called the people who came in their ship 'Bostons.' He was a great friend to the Bostons and was glad that he could trade furs for the fine things they brought in their ship. There were many, many of our people then . . . not Chinooks alone but other tribes of the Indian people, the Siwash. Every tribe was great and strong."

Debbie put her arms around Keetow and listened eagerly. For the moment, at least, she had forgotten the loss of her gun.

"After the Bostons built their fort, named Astoria, more white men came," Keetow went on. "These were the King George men, to make war. There were many more King George men than Bostons. Some came down the river. Some came from the sea in warships. My grandfather wanted to help the Bostons fight the King George men and drive them away. But the Bostons said the war was across the mountains in their own land, too. They must go back to fight it. And the King George men stayed."

The sky hung heavy and gray overhead, and rain began to spatter through the trees again. Keetow stopped. Her arms were aching. The little girl was too heavy for her to carry long. She set Debbie down, and immediately the child began to call for her little wooden gun again.

Keetow opened her bundle and drew out the doeskin dress. It would be much too large for Debbie, but it would protect her from the rain.

"See," she coaxed when Debbie had the dress on, "I will let you wear my knife. Already you wear my beautiful dress. Now you will wear my knife and belt. And you will walk a little while. I will tell you more of the story of the Siwash people as we walk.

"But not about the King George men," Keetow added. "Not about them, for they left the fort near my village and built another up the river at Vancouver. While my grandfather lived, no other Bostons came to our country.

"After Bostons left, sickness came to the Siwash." Keetow's voice sounded softly, as soft as the patter of raindrops, as soft as the padding of moccasined feet on the muddy trail. "Some blamed the Bostons for bringing the sickness. Some blamed the King George men. Some blamed evil spirits. But the blaming did not stop the dying.

"Soon some tribes were gone. The Multnomahs, who lived on the Island of Roses, were no more. The Clatsops were almost all dead. The Chinooks were weak and poor. My own father and mother died. Almost everyone had forgotten the Bostons when Jason Lee came to the valley.

"He did not come to trade. He built a house and invited the poor and hungry to stay with him. He did not call himself a Boston. He said that he was an American. In my village it was remembered that my grandfather had been a friend to those people who went back across the mountains to fight a war. The old ones decided to take me to Jason Lee's Mission to be taught and cared for. That is how I met Mrs. Garret, who is going to sail out in the ocean."

Keetow saw that Debbie was tiring. She knelt and talked the child into climbing on her back. The handsome fringe on the doeskin skirt was muddy where it dragged at the child's feet. It was sad to see the muddied dress.

"We will go to that fort they called Astoria," Keetow said in her soothing voice. "We will wave goodbye to Mrs. Garret even if she does not see us. Then I will take you back to your home. It will make your brother happy that I saved you."

Debbie was no longer listening. She was content on Keetow's back, wearing the warm, beaded dress and the knife in its sheath. But carrying her made the going very slow for the Indian girl.

Perhaps, Keetow thought, it had not been a good idea, after all, to take Debbie away with her on this journey. But if Debbie had not been along, Keetow would never have been warned of the panther!*

Keetow was bent over, climbing a rising slope, her eyes fastened on the trail. She was panting at every step. Debbie had been humming happily. Suddenly she was silent. Keetow felt her small body go rigid, then—

"Kitty!" Debbie called in a soft, coaxing voice.

Keetow looked up to see a great yellow mountain cat stretched on a limb not ten feet ahead. The girl had never seen a panther before, but she recognized that this creature was a terrible danger.

She plunged, unthinkingly, headlong into the tangle of brush and tall ferns beside the trail. She stumbled on in a panic, away from the trail, heedless of direction.

Debbie clutched Keetow's braids and screamed. But somehow she clung to the Indian girl's back until Keetow could run no more. Keetow dropped in a heap, still struck with panic, still shaking with fear. Debbie landed on all fours and scrambled up, too surprised to cry. She looked at the older girl, facedown in the fir needles. Then she came close and sat beside Keetow. She patted her thin, trembling shoulders in the same motherly way she used to pat her stick doll.

---

cougar

CHAPTER 8
The Old Tuality Trail

Tackett's pace slowed as the trail grew steeper. Still clearly marked, the way climbed through forest. Great trees shut out the sky, and fern and underbrush were shoulder-high on either side. Fallen leaves, fir needles, and rain-flattened ferns covered the trail. On such surface, moccasin prints could scarcely be seen, and Tackett was not alarmed that he had found none of Keetow's or Debbie's tracks for some time.

The forest opened briefly where a small creek crossed the trail. Here the floor of the trail was sand; surely he would find footprints. Tackett bent and searched carefully.

He saw the deep prints of a deer and the small round pad marks of some other animal, but there was nothing to show that Debbie or Keetow had passed this way. Puzzled, Tackett looked back along the trail. Plainly they had not come this far. They could not have crossed the six feet of open ground without leaving a sign.

"Perhaps," he thought, "they have turned off somewhere to camp for the night." They wouldn't be too far off the trail if that were so. If he went back slowly, calling now and then, they might hear him. Or Keetow might have a fire. He would watch for the glow of it as he retraced his steps.

It was a lonely thing to do, walking that silent trail, calling. The rain dripped heavily through the dark fir boughs, and the wet ferns brushed his legs. His voice sounded now thin, now bold, in the shadowed forest, and nothing answered it—not even the chatter of a squirrel.

By accident he found the place where Keetow had left the trail. A great tree crowded the way there, its branches low above his head. He paused a moment to lean his musket against it, to wipe the rain water from his eyes, to call and listen. His shoes were sodden, and a stone had worked its way in. As he bent to remove it, his eye was caught by a bit of brightness on the broken end of a bush. Beads! Indian beads on a few inches of thread.

Surely they had been ripped from Keetow's doeskin dress.

He picked them from the bush, his weariness forgotten in sudden excitement. Now he saw that the underbrush showed signs of having been disturbed. It looked as if Keetow had gone plunging off the trail here, fighting her way through the thick growth. Had something frightened her? Or had she heard him coming on the trail behind her and dashed into hiding? Was she hiding from him?

If that were so, his calling was of no use. Debbie might try to answer, but Keetow could easily prevent that.

For the first time, Tackett felt anger at the Indian girl. Before this he had blamed himself because he had

remarked, in front of Keetow, that he ought to take Debbie and run away. He had added some foolishness about not having a tribe to run to. Keetow might have thought from that that he wanted Debbie taken away.

But if she were hiding from him, too, it made things different. Taking up his gun again, he followed the girl's broken trail into the forest.

A half hour later, the traders bound for the Umpqua came jingling down the trail. There were fifteen horses and thirty pack ponies bearing the traders, the French-Canadian and Indian trappers, and their families and supplies. Except for the tinkle of the bells on the horses carrying women and children, the brigade traveled silently through the misery of the rain. At the place where a great tree crowded the trail, one of the horses reared.

"Blasted beast," the brigade leader muttered and went on down the trail. Then he scowled back over his shoulder as two of the pack animals broke from the string and began plunging furiously.

"Will black night find us here?" he shouted. "Control those beasts and let us be on."

"Panther!" whispered an Indian, and hurried to bring the ponies back into the string.

Then all went jingling on, down toward the Tuality plains.

∽

At the place where Keetow and Debbie had stayed the night, Ambrose and Joe Meek came near to quarreling. Ambrose was wild to push on, dark though it was. Joe was in favor of waiting until daylight.

"There'll be little sign left after that brigade went by," he pointed out. "I can't read trail by pitch light."

"The trail looks plain enough. All we have to do is follow it," Ambrose said. Worry was making him impatient with Joe Meek and his sign-reading. He kicked at the small heap of cooking stones Keetow had left and said bitterly, "I'm beginning to wonder if they were over here at all."

"They were," the mountain man answered. "And the boy was here some hours after, but afore the brigade passed by."

Another thought worried Ambrose. "Maybe they met the brigade. Maybe the traders have taken them on ahead and are sending them to Champoeg."

"Where's Tack, then?" asked Joe. "He'd be with the girls or directly behind them. If they met the brigade, he's done so, too. He wouldn't leave Louis' canoe beached there where we found it while he went on with the Company men."

"I suppose that's right. They must be still ahead of us. Well, I'm going on, Joe, even though you camp here. I've got to be doing something, right or wrong."

Joe glanced half-wistfully toward the east. His own cabin was scarcely half a dozen miles away. His Indian wife and the two babies were there in the cabin. There was hot food, a warm bed, and comfort, while here there was only a blundering greenhorn—and worry.

"Reckon we'll need a couple more pitch lights," he sighed.

To please Ambrose, the mountain man tried to read the trail, even though it was hopelessly cut and chopped by horses' hooves. Where the fallen leaves, fir needles, and dead ferns were scattered, rain water in small deep puddles reflected the light. But of the rounded prints of moccasins or the square prints of Tackett's shoes, there was not the slightest trace.

After an hour even Ambrose admitted that there was little use in hunting for signs of them, but still he wanted to keep on. The trail at least was clearly marked with no forks; the children were almost certainly ahead. Why should precious time be wasted?

"But I don't reckon they could get far," Joe tried to reason. "That little one, I figure she'd be plumb wore-out in two, three miles, and we've covered five or so since we left the river."

"Debbie walked some when we came overland. Tackett carried her as much as he could, and so did I, but she walked a great deal, too."

Joe held his tongue. Ambrose couldn't sit and wait; that was plain. They would just have to keep going. Neither of them had eaten since morning, and his hunger made Joe think of the time in the Rocky Mountains when he'd gone five days without food. He'd started out alone, headed through the snow for Fort Crockett on the Green River, and in some way lost the hammer of his gun so he couldn't hunt.

He had been near gone when another mountain man found him bedded down for what was likely his last sleep. The dried buffalo meat old Walker handed him was the best food he ever tasted in his life. It made Joe's mouth water just remembering it.

Another time he had followed an old Indian woman for two days and two nights while she went hopping across the desert, hunting water. Not a bit of food nor a drop of water did either of them swallow all that time. Light-headed and weak, he had kept going, following that hopping old woman and riled at her for being so spry when he was about done for. She had found water, though, and he had fallen facedown in it.

Come to think of it, he got almost as wet then as he was now. One thing about this Oregon country in the winter—a man didn't have to bend down for a drink. All he had to do was look up and open his mouth.

CHAPTER 9

Grandfather Bear

Keetow and Debbie had found no shelter from the rain that second night, but at the end of the third day's tramping, Keetow found a cave. She had been following a small creek which she hoped would lead back to the trail. It ran through a high rocky canyon where the evergreens clung with a dark grimness and where the ferns and devilwood struggled for foothold between moss-covered boulders.

It was a forlorn and gloomy place in the rain. But Debbie was too tired to walk much farther, and Keetow was too tired to carry her, and their clothes were sodden wet. The cave was dry and rustling and almost warm.

Keetow soon discovered that the rustling was made by bats. As she felt about in the darkness, gathering dead leaves and bits of wood for the fire, the bats swooped past her with a silent rush of air. Their black wings appeared for an instant against the mouth of the cave, and then the frightened creatures vanished to their evening hunting.

The fire made the cave wonderfully cozy. Keetow had a brisk argument with herself before she could drive her tired body out into the cold again. But they must have cooking water and more firewood. With a fire, wolves would not come into the cave and show their green glowing eyes as they had come to the camp last night.

"Stay right here, now," Keetow warned. "Don't touch the fire, and don't try to come with me."

Debbie nodded calmly. She was taking off her moccasins. She had laid her stick doll and the new gun that Keetow had carved for her on the floor beside her, close under guard. She had lost one gun and was taking no more chances with her possessions.

Keetow made her way down the rocky wall of the canyon to the creek. She would fetch water first, then gather firewood. It would be pleasant if they could have a change of food for supper. The dried salmon was growing tiresome, but in the morning they would not even have that. There was only a scrap left.

The rain had stopped briefly. Now, suddenly, just as she reached the creek, the clouds parted and a streak of the late sunlight touched the top of the canyon. Keetow stared at the sky, rigid. The sun, the first she had seen in three days, came from the wrong direction! That was the place where the sun should rise, not where it set.

Surely the creek she had followed all day ran east, to cross the Tuality trail. If it ran west, it flowed to the ocean, and she and Debbie were completely lost.

The water trembled in the little cooking basket as she dipped it out. Her knees shook under her as she climbed the ledges of rock. Should they go on, she asked herself, or should they try to retrace their steps? How long could they go without food? What would they do if they never found the Tuality trail again?

Because of the years she had spent at the Mission, Keetow had learned none of the forest lore of her people. She was not wise in the ways of the outdoors. She was as frightened and helpless now as Mrs. Garret or any American girl would have been.

Coming back to the cave, Keetow found that Debbie had emptied her shot pouch of pebbles beside the fire and was humming her little song of contentment. Keetow's heart sank as she watched the little girl. The wonderful plan for saving them both from the terrors of the journey East no longer seemed all that wonderful.

She crouched on her heels, rocked to and fro, and wailed aloud. Debbie stared, then burst into cries of her own. They clung together, two wet little children in the shelter of the cave.

It was the feel of the small, shaking body in her arms that brought Keetow's good sense back. She felt shame for frightening Debbie and for giving way to her own fear. "Come," she said. "We are not young wolves. I am the granddaughter of a chief, and you are an American."

Keetow felt confident once more. What difference did it make if the stream ran east or west? They were not lost while they followed it, even if it took them to the ocean. The Chinook village was there somewhere beside the shore, and other tribes lived near the beaches, too. Any of them would offer help to the granddaughter of Concomley.

As for food along the way, were there not always fish in every stream? Keetow hastened to put the last of the dried salmon cooking, and then with her knife cut the fringes from the beaded doeskin dress. She had thought of a wonderful plan for making a little fish net. Before she slept she would have the fish net ready for the morning.

Just before dawn the wind changed from southeast to west. The smoke from the wet wood fire began blowing downward toward the back of the cave. It blew across Keetow's face, and she woke, coughing.

Deep in the cave she heard another cough. Half awake, she reared up and blinked toward the sound. The fire gave little light, and she could see nothing. The cough sounded again. She heard a stirring of the dead leaves, a complaining growl.

Heart pounding, she crept from the blanket and seized a brand from the fire, whipping it to flame. A black bear appeared from the depths of the cave. The smoke had woken him from his winter sleep. The beast stood not fifteen feet from Keetow, swinging his head, blinking his little red eyes.

A bear will not come near fire; Keetow kept reminding herself of that. With one foot, she kicked the smoldering wood to flame, and the big creature retreated a step. She waved the brand threateningly, and he backed a step farther. Keetow breathed a bit easier. While they had fire, she could hold the animal off. But the smoke gathering in the cave made them both cough.

Debbie wakened and sat up.

"Hush!" warned Keetow. "Grandfather Bear is visiting us."

Debbie stared at the huge, dim shape.

"Kitty," laughed Debbie, delighted.

Keetow waved the brand wildly as the bear lifted to his hind legs and stood upright, manlike. Dimly she remembered an ancient bit of Chinook lore: the black bear was kin to the Siwash. Because of this, an Indian killed bear only when he could find no other food. And a bear avoided attacking the Indian unless he found himself cornered.

"If only," the girl whispered, "this bear remembers, too!"

Clutching Debbie's arm with one hand and the fire brand with the other, Keetow backed to the wall of the cave. She left a clear path to the outdoors between themselves and the fire. "Now," she said, "go, Grandfather Bear!"

As if he understood exactly what she meant, he dropped to four feet again, coughed once more, and charged speedily to the cave opening where he disappeared in the mist of the gray dawn.

"Kitty!" said Debbie regretfully.

The Indian girl's laugh was shaky with relief. "No. That is not a kitty, little yellow-hair. It is my grandfather, but not the same as Chief Concomley."

It was too late to sleep longer, and there was no breakfast to prepare. Keetow and Debbie gathered their belongings and left the cave as soon as the bear was given time to get a safe distance away. In spite of being hungry, in spite of the gloom of a thick, low-hanging fog, Keetow felt almost lighthearted. The encounter with the bear had given her a feeling of power.

She dipped her little fishing net again and again into the pools of the creek. She had made it very neatly with strips of doeskin fastened between two sides of a forked stick. But fine as it was, the fish net wouldn't catch fish. After an hour of effort, she admitted that she had ruined the beautiful dress for nothing. The net was no better than her bare hands.

Throwing it aside, she began overturning rocks at the water's edge, hunting crayfish. Debbie thought that was

wonderful fun and threw rocks with furious eagerness that would surely have frightened the little creatures into the open—if any had been there.

"Downstream, where the water is deeper, perhaps we will find a salmon so fat and heavy with eggs it cannot swim fast," Keetow said hopefully.

She hurried Debbie on down the creek. At the bend, however, they found that the canyon narrowed and they must climb to a ledge which skirted the rock wall fifty feet above.

Debbie climbed bravely, with Keetow behind. "Careful," the Indian girl cautioned as they edged along the high path. "I am glad that we did not meet Grandfather Bear here. He could not have turned about to run from us."

Suddenly she stopped and stood very still, listening. Surely that had been a voice calling. A thin voice, not far away. She looked at the cliff above and saw only the gray, threatening wall rising into the blue of the clearing sky. Below, she saw nothing except a scarred place on the moss of the sharply sloping boulders just above the creek. A stick caught between two boulders looked very black against the white mist that still steamed from the water.

She told herself that the voice had been a bird call or the cry of some animal. She started onward with Debbie again. But that cry had sounded strangely human. There! It came again. It came from below.

Once more she leaned over the rough wall of the canyon. That black stick caught her attention. It seemed to glint dully, like metal ... like a gun barrel.

Her eyes narrowed intently; there was something white beside the gun barrel stick. Was it a hand?

"Debbie," she whispered, "someone is lying there, hurt. I—I believe it is your brother."

CHAPTER 10
Signal Smoke

"Do I have to tell you how to make smoke signals?" asked Tackett. "You're the Indian."

Keetow hung her head. "I do not know if my Chinook people had such a custom," she said. "I am sorry."

Tackett began to be ashamed of himself. He had never in his life been so glad to see anyone as Keetow and Debbie. Yet he had been scolding almost steadily since the moment they came into view around the boulder that pinned his foot. First, he yelled at Keetow because she couldn't move the stone to free him. Then, he had blamed her for taking Debbie away and making so much trouble.

And all the while the Indian girl kept tugging at the stone, bringing him water or tucking her blanket under him so the rocks wouldn't cut so sharply. She had not tried to defend or excuse herself at all. He noticed now that she had put that beaded dress she was so proud of on Debbie.

Of the two girls, Debbie looked considerably fresher and better fed. Keetow had taken good care of his little sister.

"I guess you wouldn't have a chance to learn many Indian ways, living at the Mission so long," he said. "But smoke-signaling is easy. You just need a good smoky fire and a blanket. We can't really spell out anything, but if we get a good line of smoke and keep interrupting it, most anybody would come and see what the trouble was.

"Pa will be hunting us by this time, and maybe Joe Meek is with him," Tackett said bravely. Though it did seem as if Joe would have found their trail sooner. Joe was the best tracker in the country. It wouldn't take him nearly so long to cut Keetow and Debbie's trails as it had taken Tackett. Nor would he run beyond it, as Tackett had, and get caught between two rolling boulders at the bottom of a canyon.

Tackett still didn't understand quite how that had happened. It had been almost dark when he got into the canyon. He was just poking around, looking for a camp place, when he smelled the smoke of Keetow's fire. Though he could smell it, he had not been able to see the glow. He had gone on, excited and calling, hunting for the fire that had to be there. Suddenly he had heard something above him. He knew it was a slide of stone coming down the cliff, but it was too dark to see where it was aiming. He hadn't known which way to dodge. He had run headlong into the sliding boulders and fallen.

For about two hours afterwards, he had told himself how blessed he was that the rock hadn't crushed him. But as the night wore on, he had wondered if it wouldn't have been better to have been killed outright. With his foot

caught between those big rocks, he would starve or freeze to death before he was discovered.

Then he had heard Keetow and Debbie on the ledge above him and had managed to call them. Debbie sat beside him now, patting his head. She looked into his face anxiously. "Milk?" she asked. "Milk, Tacky?"

"She is hungry," Keetow said, low-voiced. "I had no food for her breakfast."

Tackett had no food either. Gravely they discussed how they could find something to eat. A wild duck flew by, close to the water, and Tackett lifted his head to watch it longingly. "I've still got a charge of powder," he said. "And my gun didn't take any damage when I fell—but I don't suppose you can shoot."

"If you would tell me—" Keetow hesitated.

"You might hit a bear if you held the muzzle to his head," Tackett answered. "No use wasting the powder on anything moving."

"I could not shoot a bear, for they are of my family."

Why couldn't she remember some Indian stuff that was useful, Tackett reflected gloomily. "If you can make a fire," he said, "I'll tell you how to signal."

Keetow built the fire on the slope of the bank below Tackett so that he could hold one corner of the signal blanket. Debbie held another corner, and Keetow the opposite two. A signaler usually needed no help. But Keetow was not tall enough nor strong enough to whip the heavy wool over the fire and back again with the quick, sharp motions that cut the smoke in two.

Debbie soon tired of the game and dropped her corner in spite of all coaxing. Determinedly she scrambled down to the creek to enjoy the more exciting pleasure of throwing rocks into the water. Tackett found his arms growing weary, and Keetow panted and perspired as smoke rose in broken white puffs.

"Somebody is sure to see that," grunted Tackett. "There isn't a whisper of wind to blow it away."

But the lack of wind was a worry, too. The quiet, cold air promised frost, maybe a real freeze. Caught there between the rocks, Tackett had been cold enough the night before. He wondered if he could stand another night even colder.

"You and Debbie better go back to the cave tonight," he told Keetow. "No use staying out here when you've got shelter closeby."

"We will stay," she answered firmly.

A shriek rose from Debbie at the water's edge. "Kitty!" she cried joyfully. "Kitty!"

Keetow whirled. "The bear. Grandfather Bear has returned!"

But it wasn't the bear. A porcupine was ambling along the shore, head-down, indifferent to any other creature that might be foolish enough to touch it.

"Food!" shouted Tackett. "Keetow, anybody can kill a porcupine! Grab a piece of that fire wood, quickly, and crack him one behind the head."

Four days, thought Ambrose. Four long days and four longer nights had passed since Debbie and Tackett had been gone. Could the little girl possibly be alive? He thought of hunger and cold and wild beasts, of the wolves howling at night. The sound chilled his heart with fear for the children.

It seemed as if everything had gone against Joe Meek and Ambrose in their search. First, the brigade had destroyed any traces of the children on the Tuality trail. Then, the group of settlers had come, meaning to be helpful, but only further trampling down the underbrush.

Joe had been forced to cast far wide of the trail, foot by foot on either side for a dozen miles before he picked up the first hint. And then it was Tackett's prints he found—Tackett's alone.

"What about it?" Joe asked. "Follow the boy, or keep hunting the girls' trail?"

"Tack left the main trail for some reason," Ambrose said. "He must have known that Debbie and Keetow left it hereabouts and turned off after them. I believe we should follow him."

Joe shook his head doubtfully, but he was uncertain himself, so he followed Ambrose's advice. The boy's tracks led them back and forth through the forest for a whole day before the print of Keetow's and Debbie's moccasins came into Joe Meek's vision. They had lost almost a day, for Tackett had wandered that long before he stumbled—accidentally it must have been—across the trail of the girls.

"Can't help admirin' that Indian girl," Joe said. "She's headed for the coast the most direct way."

"But does she know where she's going?" Ambrose asked.

Joe shrugged and forged ahead without answering. Ambrose thought of Mrs. Garret, who had come up to the Tuality trail with two men from the Mission. She had brought loaves of bread, a roast quarter of meat, and a great iron kettle of coffee to feed the men who had gathered to help with the search.

Her eyes were red from crying, and it was all the men could do to keep her from starting out through the woods at Joe Meek's heels to hunt for Keetow. She had scolded

Ambrose for his anger at the Indian girl. "She's only a child herself!" Mrs. Garret exclaimed. "I am the one to blame. I should never have tried to force her to go East with me."

"I thought it was best for her, too," Ambrose admitted.

"I was sure she would enjoy the journey, once it was begun," Mrs. Garret mourned. "And it would have been such a help to the Mission. Keetow would have proved to everyone that we have helped the Indians, that many have learned to love God and read His word. Besides," she said, "I love Keetow. I meant to adopt her if I found she was happy in Boston."

You had to admire a woman like that, thought Ambrose as he trotted along after Joe. She had given her youth, her husband, and her heart to this missionary work among the Oregon Indians. Few women that he had known would have the courage to adopt a little Indian girl and try to make her happy in an Eastern city.

Joe stopped to study some faint marks on the mossy rocks at the head of a canyon. "Tack wasn't far behind the girls here," he said.

"How far is Tackett ahead of us?" Ambrose asked.

Joe looked up as if he didn't understand how anybody could be so blind to plain marked signs. "He was here evenin' before last."

"How can you tell?"

"Rain let up then. Up-creek a quarter mile, Tack's prints were rain-washed. Here they aren't."

"Then there's no hope that we'll find them today," Ambrose groaned. "It does seem to me that two men could travel faster than a twelve-year-old girl burdened with a baby."

"Keetow don't have to hunt trail," Joe said.

Ambrose's impatience was wearing his nerves. The man didn't understand tracking, and he fretted at Joe every time they had to delay a minute.

Joe was beginning to wish he'd left Ambrose on the trail with Mrs. Garret and the other greenhorns.

He stood up and stretched. He was getting soft here in the Oregon country, living in a cabin, leading a settler's life. Two, three days on the trail made him creak in the joints.

Suddenly he stiffened with his arms still wide-stretched. Smoke signals, by the Great Beaver! Smoke signals, and not more than half a mile ahead!

"Reckon you'll find your young 'uns there," he said, trying to sound offhand. "Leastways, Tack will be there. Indians in these parts don't signal so."

⟿

It took two full days to bring the children back over the trail. Tackett's foot was bruised and painful, though no bones seemed to be broken. He hobbled along for the first few hours with the use of a stick and Joe Meek's helping hand. Then they were met by Louis Palette and another Canadian on Company horses.

Debbie, her adventure ended, was cross and fretful. Ambrose carried her until they reached the horses. He was so glad to find her safe and sound, he could scarcely take his eyes from her.

Keetow went along without protest. This surprised Tackett. He wondered if she had forgotten that the ship was in the river, ready to take her and Mrs. Garret to the States. If he had been in her place, he would have helped himself to some of the food supplies the men had brought and slipped away. She was already halfway home. She could have got to her own people before the men were free to search for her.

But maybe she no longer wanted to escape. Of course, she had had a rough time with Debbie. The rain and cold, the bear and the panther, might have made her decide she'd rather go with Mrs. Garret than spend more time in the wilderness. But he didn't really believe she was thinking of the dangers.

He watched her pretty closely whenever he thought she wasn't noticing. And she didn't notice much. She trudged along with her head down and her feet dragging—tired, like the rest of them.

But she had a gray look and a dullness in her eyes that seemed more than tiredness. Had she taken cold last night when she wouldn't go to the cave? Debbie had slept cuddled up next to him under his blanket. It wasn't until half the night was gone that he had realized he had Keetow's blanket folded under him. She had been poking around with the fire, and he'd gone to sleep without thinking of the blanket.

Anybody with any sense would have spoken up, reminding him that she needed it, Tackett told himself crossly. But likely she had an idea that a good Indian didn't complain. He supposed he owed his life to Keetow. But she had been to blame, too, for getting him into such a fix in the first place, taking Debbie away and then leaving the trail.

Of course, she did take good care of him until his father and Joe Meek got there to free him from the trap he was in. Sooner or later, he was going to have to thank her. But right now, he just hoped she wasn't feeling as sick as she looked.

CHAPTER 11

Darkened Cabin

The calf was gone. The longhorn's lonely cry sounded from the corral as the party neared home. The cow had held off the wolves but had been too slow to stop a panther's silent leap.

Bear, panther, wolf—the wild beasts were growing bolder as they discovered the easy prey in pens and corrals behind the settlers' cabins. All up and down the valley it was the same; men felt despairing rage as they counted the cost of midnight raids.

It was so difficult to get a start in raising farm animals here. A man might work a month to pay for a lamb, then lose it in a night. Another couldn't be bought at any price. A clutch of eggs might be worth more to a man than having his wheat fields fenced. He could build the fence himself, but he couldn't get more eggs.

The French-Canadians were responsible to the Company for the livestock loaned them and were bound to return to the Company farms the increase of the animals. They were hardest hit. They expected to lose a calf or young goat or two to wild beasts, but during no other winter had they counted such losses. Angrily they blamed the Americans. The new settlers had killed so many rabbits, game birds, deer, and other natural prey, they had driven the flesh eaters to invade the farmyards.

The Canadians were not hunters. Their ancient Company muskets collected rust above the fireplaces, and they had no urge to begin hunting in the wet forests.

The day after Tackett's homecoming, Louis Palette pointed out a heap of bones and scrap of red hide, all that was left of the long-legged little calf. "Marie say another pig gone also," he wailed. "I give your papa powder. Why he not hunt that killer?"

Tackett shook his head. A worse killer than panther was on his mind just now. "I'll hunt it myself, soon as I can walk easy," he said indifferently.

Louis glanced up. "Your papa not change his mind about send little one on ship?" he asked.

"I guess he'll send her if Mrs. Garret goes. But Keetow's pretty sick, and Mrs. Garret won't leave her."

"I think Keetow pretend sick, maybe," Louis winked.

That had been Tackett's idea, at first. He had thought that Keetow had figured out another way to avoid boarding the ship with Mrs. Garret. But now it was plain that the Indian girl was really ill.

"Mrs. Garret and Joe Meek brought her to our cabin this morning," he said. "They think she's got measles."

"Measles!" Louis whispered.

Tackett watched the fear whiten Louis' face. "Is it that bad?" he asked. "Debbie and I had measles last spring, and I don't remember being so sick. But Mrs. Garret acts scared to death for Keetow."

"For Indian it is very bad. For my Marie and my children, it is very bad."

Louis Palette spoke truly. Scarcely one out of a hundred Indians struck down by measles survived. In the Tuality lodge where Keetow had spent a night ten days before, the little boy was dead and the baby would be dead before another morning. In the Brandts' cabin, Mrs. Garret had despairingly begged for a bed for Keetow. She had asked for the warmest, cleanest of the blankets, for medicines and tea, and almost complete darkness.

Ambrose tiptoed clumsily about the cabin, trying to provide the things Mrs. Garret needed to nurse the sick girl. He understood that she couldn't keep Keetow at Joe Meek's cabin any longer. She couldn't take her to the Mission—other children had to be considered. His cabin was one of the few where the Indian girl could be cared for without too great a risk of spreading the sickness.

Outside, Joe Meek worked on a lean-to, which Ambrose had hastily begun when he saw that he and Tackett would have to move outside. Joe disliked cabin-building almost as much as he disliked plowing. "Being neighborly fetches me more trouble," he muttered, "than fleas on a dog."

⌇

The worst of it all was the feeling of uselessness that possessed everyone while Keetow lay ill. Ambrose found a remarkable number of weeds which he must pull in the wheat field, though nothing else seemed to be growing now. Tackett cut wood enough to feed one of the new steamboats he had seen in the Ohio River. Both gloomily thought up as many outdoor chores as possible to keep them away from the cabin.

Tackett could still remember the nightmare visions that beset him when he had been ill with measles. Yet, compared to Keetow, he had hardly been sick at all. Every morning, when he slipped in to renew the wood supply and refill the water kettle, he found Mrs. Garret beside the narrow bed, sitting quietly with a helpless look on her face.

"Is she any better?" Tackett would ask.

And Mrs. Garret would answer, "I believe she is, Tackett. Yes, I'm sure she is, thank you."

Dr. Bailey came down from Champoeg, bringing other medicines. He shook his head as he came outside the cabin. "I can't understand it," he said. "Anne Garret really believes that child will survive."

He sat down on the split log bench outside the cabin door and lifted Debbie to his lap, stroking her shining yellow hair. "The ship sails tomorrow," he said. "I told Anne that, but she scarcely seemed to listen. I wonder if we ought to persuade her that she should not postpone her return to the States. The little Indian can live only a day or two, at the most."

Ambrose looked at Debbie and sighed. "I believe that Mrs. Garret has weighed the cost," he said. "There will be another ship in the spring."

Tackett dug his fists into his pockets and turned away so the men couldn't see his face. Once, he had thought he would be perfectly happy just to know that the ship would sail without Debbie—but now, well, he hadn't wanted it to happen like this.

The men stuffed their pipes and settled back for a talk. Dr. Bailey had recently attended a meeting of the Willamette Falls Debating Society, held in the Mission granary. The question of independent government, he said, had been argued openly. The discussion was quite heated. A few still contended that a code of laws and a militia and sheriff for enforcing the laws should be set up. They said that the Americans should set up government whether the Canadians favored it or not.

But that opinion was not held by many. Most felt that if there was to be a law at all, it had to be for everyone. If settlers' law and Company law were to try to live side by side, there would be trouble.

Ambrose was interested in the resolution that had been presented by George Abernathy, who spoke for Jason Lee and other important men of the Mission: "Resolved, that if the United States extends its jurisdiction over this country within the next four years, it will not be necessary to form an independent government."

Ambrose stroked his curly black beard. "I've not favored any hasty action," he declared, "but four years seems a long while to blunder along with no government at all. Did Abernathy's resolution go unprotested?"

"Indeed, it did not," said Dr. Bailey. "The dust fairly flew over that resolution for postponing action. Mark my words, we'll have government here, by one means or another, before this winter ends."

"May the Lord grant we gain it by peaceful means," said Ambrose. He looked toward the cabin again and sighed. "Poor Keetow. I can't get it from my mind that we're all guilty in a way—"

"Because she's dying of measles? Nonsense, man. The natives haven't the power to fight sickness that we have. How could you be to blame for that? I think you have been overly forgiving to that Indian girl. After all, she did steal your daughter away." Dr. Bailey impatiently stood up and clapped his pipe against the bench. "I must go on," he said. "I've promised to take a book to Louis Palette. I find I am becoming one of the circulating library's agents."

"Is Louis a member of the library? I didn't know he could read English," Ambrose said.

"Yes, indeed. I'm taking him the *History of the American Revolution*. That was the only book left on the shelves. The committee has collected money to buy new books. Louis and Etienne Lucier were among the first to bring their dollars. But until the new books arrive, they must read what we have."

Ambrose smiled with the doctor. "I do believe that the library has done more to bring us together than any idea we've had so far. If we could think up something else—some reason why the Canadians should band together with us—we might lead them to see that organizing would be to the advantage of all of us."

"Play-acting—something like that, perhaps?" suggested the doctor.

"That wouldn't please the Mission, I'm afraid. Besides, I think it should be something more serious. If we could think of something that concerns the welfare of the Canadians, yet isn't handled for them by the Company, they might join our plans for government."

Tackett, who had been listening quietly, spoke up. "Louis Palette wants us to kill the wolves and panthers for him. He's mighty concerned about that."

Ambrose, half-listening, nodded. "Yes, that's right, son. Well, Dr. Bailey, we will think of something, I am sure."

The doctor stepped into his skiff and took up his oars. "By the way, an old Chinook brought that little blue dugout of Keetow's to Champoeg when he heard she was sick. It's not likely she'll ever get well to use it, though it might do to bury her in. That's an old Chinook custom, you know."

Tackett stood with clenched fists, watching the man pull away upstream. Why should the doctor be so sure that Keetow would die? Mrs. Garret didn't believe it, and now, suddenly Tackett knew that he didn't believe it either. He would go and bring back the canoe, but not to bury Keetow in. It would be there, moored at their own landing, when she was ready to use it again.

CHAPTER 12
This Government Business

Tackett had not meant to stop at Champoeg longer than to get the canoe. As he pulled his skiff in to the landing, however, the sound of a big familiar voice sent him scrambling up the high river bank. Joe Meek's booming voice came from the granary building, and he sounded as angry as if he had put his head in a wasp's nest.

Tackett had just put his hand to the granary door when he heard a bellow of a rage and another shout. The door burst open. Tackett barely had time to jump aside as a struggling huddle of men lurched out. They were holding Joe aloft with his big feet thrashing the air higher than his head. He had lost his hat, his long hair streamed wildly, and his voice might have been heard at the Mission fifteen miles away.

"Them's prime beaver!" he was shouting.

His swinging arm caught a Canadian on the ear, and the man howled and let go his grip. The others heaved, and Joe went sliding into the mud. Before he could gain his feet, they had scrambled back inside the trading post and slammed the door.

Joe cocked his head and grinned at Tackett.

"That's three times they done this. You figure maybe I ain't welcome, Tack?"

"Have you been trying to trade beaver?" Tackett asked in awe.

Joe winked. "They allow I have."

His wide black hat came sailing through a quickly opened crack of the trading-house door. Joe bent to pick it up and wiped the mud from it with his sleeve. "Reckon I'm gettin' old," he sighed. "It only took five of them to toss me out of there."

"I counted six," Tackett said kindly.

Joe walked to the door and gave it a final, crashing kick, then turned away. "Five, six—no difference. Must be I'm getting old."

"I'll help you if you want to try it again."

Joe shook his head. "I've had my fun."

"What about your furs? Are they still inside?"

The door opened again, and a fur pack dropped at Joe's feet. "There's your beaver," an angry voice called. "Next time you take Company fur, you'll get worse than we gave you today."

Joe laughed soundlessly all the way down to the landing. When he tossed the fur pack into his skiff, it burst open, and Tackett understood the laughter. Inside the pack were no beaver pelts but a wolf skin and a tattered old buffalo hide. Joe had been taunting the Company agent again, but this time had saved himself the work of trapping.

"I was scared he might open the pack," Joe said. "'Twould have been his laugh, if he had."

Tackett lifted the wolf pelt. "You killed this just lately, didn't you?"

"I got three from a band that were runnin' my wife's pony. If we could eat wolf, we'd all be fat."

Joe's eyes had a worried look behind the laughter, and Tackett wondered suddenly if he were having trouble keeping his family fed. Joe could bring in game when he had powder, but the garden patch beside his cabin was the poorest in the valley. He owned no livestock except the pony. It might be that Joe and his family had nothing but boiled wheat to eat most of the time.

"You could fish," Tackett blurted.

"I could farm, too," retorted Joe, "if I were different than I be. Someways, Tack, I am plumb a failure." He looked away toward the hills. "I get hungry for the mountains and the way it used to be. Livin' just for the day, glad when beaver were plenty, not frettin' when it weren't." He broke off and sighed. "But it's gone. The Sublette boys don't pack to the mountains no more. Kit, ,Carson, Bridger—where are they? Like the preacher says, I've set my hand to the plow. Reckon it'll have to stay there, if I want it or not."

Tackett, awkward with a new sympathy for the free-hearted man he had always admired, had a thought. "I know a job you could do, Joe! You'd make a real good sheriff. You wouldn't have to do much of any work, just go around hunting anybody who committed a crime. Why, there isn't a man in the valley would make a better sheriff."

"I'd like that," Joe said thoughtfully. "But there can't be a sheriff without law, and there can't be law without gover'ment. Seems like folks have lost interest since the Canadians voted us down. They are settin' back, swapping readin' books and hopin' John McLoughlin will forget they signed petitions. Can't even get anybody to call a meetin'. They say we have palavered everything there was to fret us and done not a bit of good."

"They haven't talked about wolves!" Tackett said suddenly.

"Wolves?" asked Joe, puzzled. "What's there to say for wolves?"

"Everybody's complaining about them," Tackett pointed out. "You want to get the settlers together; why don't you ask them to join up to clean out the wolves and panthers? Even the Canadians would be glad to have you do that."

"Reckon they'd approve, all right," Joe nodded. "But I don't see as it would forward gover'ment."

"Pa didn't think much of the idea either," Tackett admitted. "Maybe it's not any good."

As Joe stepped into his skiff, he noticed the blue canoe tied behind Tackett's boat for towing. "I'm plumb sorry that child got measles," he said. "She was a plucky little girl. White man's sickness shouldn't have beat her."

Tackett tightened his lips. "Keetow isn't dead. Mrs. Garret thinks she's better."

"There's no such thing as better when an Indian gets measles," Joe answered. "Smallpox, measles, either one is sure death. I can't scarcely believe she's hung on this long."

"Maybe this once it'll be different," said Tackett, and he pulled quickly out into the current. He didn't want to hear, even from Joe Meek, that Mrs. Garret was waging a hopeless fight for Keetow's life.

But as he walked up to the cabin from the landing an hour later, he was struck by the sharp fear that Joe had been right. The cabin door was closed, Ambrose and Debbie were nowhere in sight, and the stillness of the clearing seemed somehow frightening.

Cautiously he pushed the door open and looked inside. An ache came to his throat as he saw Mrs. Garret on her knees beside Keetow's bed, her face in her hands. In the dimness of the room, the whisper of her voice was a prayer, and the face of the Indian girl was smooth and peaceful.

Grief and angry protest struck at Tackett. Keetow shouldn't have lost the fight—it wasn't fair. His knees trembled as he moved forward. Keetow opened her eyes and looked at him. "There is mud on your face," she said clearly. "It is not good to be dirty."

Mrs. Garret smiled through her tears. "Her fever is gone. She is better—I've been thanking God—"

The ache in Tackett's throat got bigger; he couldn't even swallow. Turning on his heel, he dashed out-of-doors as fast as he could go. Debbie would want to hear this news—Debbie and his father!

⁓

The cabin had a lonesome feeling after Keetow and Mrs. Garret went back to the Mission. Debbie kept asking for one or the other of them, and once or twice before Christmas, Ambrose took her to visit them.

There wasn't much else to do but visit during these short rain-filled winter days. There was nothing to be done outside, and a man could work only so long at fixing up the inside of a cabin.

Though there were no big political meetings during that winter, the subject of government was talked over at every fireside. Men traveled the long wet miles between cabin and cabin to spend an hour with one another, to talk over their problems or grope for new ideas.

Many visitors came to the Brandt cabin. Though Ambrose was almost a newcomer to the valley, his grave, thoughtful opinions were already valued. Men of importance sought him out. They realized that his point of view might be more valuable than that of someone who had been in the political struggle from the first.

Men from the Mission liked to talk with Ambrose, too. Jason Lee and the other missionaries were interested in government, and they liked a good argument.

All his life Tackett would recall the talk he heard that winter while he sat with Debbie in a corner of the cabin. He would watch the leaping fire and listen as rain beat on the roof and wind howled about the log walls. He never forgot the sound of his father's quiet voice explaining over and over why he considered an independent government dangerous.

"It could too easily be controlled by the Britishers. They have more votes than we do. No, sir, I believe that whatever we do to establish government, we must make it American." Patiently he sought for words to express his thought. "We transplanted settlers are making the future. What we do will control the treaty between the two countries for the northwest boundary. We must openly advance the claim of the United States, as Hudson's Bay Company's efforts here have advanced Great Britain's claim."

That was the heart of the matter, Tackett realized. It wasn't simply a matter of how the wheat weighed, or whether the Company could claim all the beaver. The important decision was whether this fair, green land should stay under the British flag or if the Stars and Stripes would reach from sea to sea.

"But if we can't get them to vote for any kind of government, how can we expect a vote that will support the United States?" one man argued. "Especially when we get no encouragement from Congress?"

That was the stumbling block on which each discussion tripped. No one knew how to overcome the Canadians' solid vote of "no."

It was a pleasant surprise to learn that one Canadian was more than ready to join with the Americans. Louis Palette brought the man to meet Ambrose.

"Francois Mathieu say he wish to be American," Louis laughed. "I tell him then he should know M'sieu Brandt, for M'sieu Brandt and his friends very much wish to stay American."

Mathieu had been mixed up in a French rebellion against British rule in Canada during the 1830s. That rebellion of the French Canadians had failed. Mathieu had escaped to the States and come to Oregon to make his home. He was bitter against British rule in Canada and strong in his sympathy with the neighboring country.

"Aren't you afraid he'll persuade you to join us, Louis?" asked Ambrose with a rare twinkle in his eyes.

"When government make me pay tax on each door and window in my cabin, I think government no good," Louis answered moodily. "Company agent say that is what your law do."

"Have they been telling you that?" Ambrose's smile faded. "Louis, it isn't true. You will have a say in any tax levied. Didn't you read in the history book you got from the circulating library that 'taxation without representation' was one of the reasons for the American Revolution? When we have government, you will vote for representatives to levy your taxes for you."

"I read it." Louis nodded. "But I do not like tax even when I vote it. Under Company I pay none."

"Under the Company you are like a child. Even your land is yours only so long as McLoughlin says so. Your children will grow up the same, cared for, protected, yes—but bound to the Company just as you are."

Louis' dark glance flashed. "Without Company, I have no land at all. I do not own paper to say your Congress give me square mile in Oregon."

"Those papers don't give land to us either. Congress hasn't passed the Linn bill and may never do so. One of the reasons that I favor the establishment of a provisional government is that we will have jurisdiction over land claims. Who is there now to say if the claim at Willamette

Falls belongs to Dr. McLoughlin, or to Alvin Waller, who has set buildings on the land? Or to the Indians who have fished there for so many years?"

"What is this provisional government?" asked Francois Mathieu. "I have not before heard of it."

"It's an idea some of us have talked about. A provisional government would answer our present needs. It would be independent in the sense that we've set it up ourselves. Yet it would stand only as a bridge to the time when Congress decides if we are to become part of the States."

"If your Congress decide Oregon is not worth war with England, what your little government do?" sneered Louis.

"It might become a big government," Ambrose said gravely. "Who knows?"

"Not so big as Company," Louis shrugged and turned to point a finger at Tackett. "Why you do not hunt panther, as you promise?" he asked.

"I hunted it," said Tackett. "The hide is stretched in the lean-toif you want to take a look."

"Must be he have brother," Louis grunted. "They take my children next time, maybe."

Francois Mathieu shook his head. "My friend, Pierre Beleque, complain that wolves make bold with his farmyard. Yet he does not hunt these animals."

"Everybody's waiting for his neighbor to do it," said Tackett, teasing Louis.

Ambrose started to frown at him, then stared intently, sudden understanding in his look.

"The wolves—the wolves and the panthers," he murmured. "You are right, Tack. Everyone is interested in getting rid of the wild beasts. I believe a meeting to wage war on the wolves might be very well attended."

CHAPTER 13

Wolf Meeting

The first "Wolf Meeting" was called for February 2, 1843. Word of it was carried from cabin to cabin up and down the valley. Hudson's Bay Company men, missionaries, and settlers alike heard the news with interest and approval. At last something was to be done about protecting the valuable livestock.

It was not certain how many knew of the secret purpose behind the meeting. No one liked to speak of it directly, for the other person might not know or he might not approve. He might let something slip where Company ears could hear it.

The meeting was well attended by both Americans and Canadians. The meeting was called to order by the Reverend I.L. Babcock, who announced that the object of the meeting was to adopt some measures for the protection of their herds and livestock.

Smoothly William Gray moved that a committee of six be appointed to study the matter and prepare a report. The motion was seconded immediately.

The chairman appointed to the committee an equal number of Canadians and Americans. The meeting closed in a spirit of friendliness and neighborliness. There was not a whisper of argument; the distressing subject of government was not mentioned. Everyone left the gathering with a fine feeling that something had been done. They were eager to hear what the committee would tell them when they met again March 4th.

"But they didn't do anything," protested Tackett to Joe Meek later. "Now we've got to wait a whole month—and the wolves are still roaming the clearings."

"The louder they howl, the happier the Canadians'll be to get organized." Joe winked broadly. "Remember, Tack, it ain't only wolves we're after, it's gover'ment. We have got to coax these people, easy-like. When you are aimin' to hoist something heavier than you be, make sure your hoist lever is wedged in proper. Huntin' wolves is our lever, and we're sure wedgin' it in."

Joe was growing a beard and had cut his hair. He didn't look so much like a mountain man any more. He still wore his buckskins, but they were so patched and short of fringe he would have been ashamed to wear them in the Rocky Mountains.

"Reckon I'll have to get a new suit when I'm sheriff," he said. "Wouldn't look right, a big man like a sheriff walkin' around in worn-out buckskin."

"Don't count your chickens," Tackett grinned.

Joe fixed him with a dark look. "These are prairie chicken, son, and Joe Meek's got a bead plumb on them."

The last two weeks in February were bright and almost warm. The green sprouts of wheat began to lengthen. The woods were carpeted with pale, star-like flowers, and in the unplowed fields the Indian root, camas, stirred and reached for the light. The rivers swelled with the first melting of snow from the mountains, and the little creeks that had been rain-fed dropped an inch or two.

Webb Heathwire came visiting Tackett again, wanting to know how to apply that wrestling hold. Tackett was forced to refuse. It wasn't that he wanted to keep it a secret, but that he didn't know himself how he had gotten Webb down. The wrestling hold had been an accident, pure and simple.

"That hold is a dangerous thing to know, Webb," he explained airily. "Can't let everybody in on information like that or we'd have a bunch of busted arms all over the Oregon country."

Webb admitted that was right. But he promised that he would be mighty careful how he applied the hold and to whom. His brother, now—Webb thought his life might be considerably eased if his brother had a broken arm.

Tackett refused to be persuaded. Then Webb turned to the subject of the "wolf committee." "They're fixin' to pay bounties on the skins," he said. "Pa says a fellow could make himself rich on the bounties they're fixin' to pay for pelts."

"How do you know so much what they're planning to do?" asked Tackett a little resentfully. He had been the one to suggest organizing to wage war on the wild beasts. Everyone seemed to have forgotten that now, and he had not been told any of the committee's plans. "It's supposed to be a secret report until the meeting," he blurted out.

"That Frenchie, Lucier, told Pa. Pa says iffen I want, I can just spend my time wolf-huntin.'"

"What about powder?" Tackett asked.

"Everybody can get it now but them as thought up the petition. Pa signed, but he never thought up none of the mean things it said about Dr. McLoughlin."

Tackett's father hadn't even signed the petition; he had not been in Oregon when it was drawn up. If they could get powder now, at Hudson's Bay Company, Tackett could collect some bounties, too. He scanned the woods thoughtfully. The bounty ought to be at least fifty cents an animal, and at that rate, if he killed ten wolves—

The answer pleased him so much he felt a wave of good will which included even Webb. "You can hunt with me if you want to," he said. "We can split what we get."

Webb hesitated. "You figurin' on takin' that little girl to hunt?"

Tackett wasn't intending to; wolf-hunting was too dangerous for Debbie, but he wouldn't admit it to Webb. "She usually goes with me," he said firmly.

"Well," sighed Webb, "I reckon I can stand having her along iffen you can."

⁓

Keetow dipped the paddle of the little blue canoe with measured, careful strokes. The river was very high and fast now, and an upset could be dangerous. Mrs. Garret sat on a folded blanket in the prow of the canoe, holding gifts for the Brandt family clutched in her hands. Keetow looked at the older woman solemnly. She was bound now to Mrs. Garret; her life belonged to the woman who had given it back to her—no more rebellion, no more running away. Her footsteps must follow Mrs. Garret's wherever they led.

The girl no longer thought of the journey East with fear, yet still she was sad because she must go. Her eyes returned to the river. Perhaps it was this that she did not want to leave—the river and the canoes, the wild rains and the soft sunlight. No other place could be like this. No other place could be so beautiful.

She thrust her paddle deeper and swung the light craft toward the mouth of the creek. Mrs. Garret smiled, and Keetow smiled in return.

They reached the Brandt cabin at exactly the right time, considering the gift that Keetow had brought. Tackett was struggling to put a leather patch over the cut-out toe of his boot. Keetow held out her gift of moccasins, and the boy took them with a shout of pleasure.

"I've been wanting some like Debbie's," he said. "I never thought my feet would be comfortable again."

Ambrose was as pleased with the soft woolen stockings Mrs. Garret had knitted for him, and Debbie paraded her scarlet broadcloth cape with pride.

"It's like Christmas," smiled Ambrose as Mrs. Garret unwrapped the last gift, a cake rich with plums and nut meats. "Much more of a Christmas than the one we managed this year."

"Mine would have been sad," Mrs. Garret said, "if you had not been kind enough to let us use your cabin when Keetow was ill. Even if a place could have been made for her at the Mission, I doubt if she could have survived many more hours of travel in the rain."

This was the moment Keetow had been waiting for. She stepped forward and modestly smoothed her skirt. "I thank you for the shelter I had in your home," she said loudly. "I am sorry I caused your hearts to ache for the little yellow-hair." As if frightened by her own voice, she

whirled and caught up a piece of cake and thrust it at Tackett. "Eat!" she ordered. "It is very good."

Tackett took a huge bite, and everyone laughed at his groan of delight. The cabin seemed very warm and pleasant when eating cake with the sun shining in through the open door.

Tackett sighed happily and leaned back to admire Debbie dancing about in her new cape. "Pretty, pretty," she was saying.

"I guess we can throw away that old jacket I made over," he remarked. "Now that Debbie's got something proper to wear."

"Oh, you mustn't let her play in it," warned Mrs. Garret. "It's for dress-up occasions—and when she goes East with Keetow and me."

Suddenly the cake was a lump in Tackett's throat. The ship! Spring was almost here, and the ship was due some time early in May. Although so much had happened during the winter, nothing had happened, really, to change his father's intention of sending Debbie East with Mrs. Garret.

Tackett studied the toe of his moccasin while the silence lengthened. He could feel his father's eyes on him, waiting for him to make a fuss. His father was already gathering up his arguments to prove why it was best for Debbie to go—like the Americans, trying to prove to the Canadians that self-government was important! The Canadians couldn't see it, but when you were on the other side, the truth was plain.

"Come here, Debbie," said Tackett, stern with misery. "Come here and let me hang your cape away. You've got to keep it clean for the trip."

⌒

The second wolf meeting was held on the 6th of March in the home of Joseph Gervais, one of the settlers living

near Champoeg. The chairman called the meeting to order and asked for the report of the "wolf committee." Applause, murmurs of praise, and agreement greeted each resolution of the "wolf committee's" report.

As was expected, the committee proposed "immediate measures for the destruction of all wolves, panthers, and bears, and such other animals as are known to be dangerous to cattle, horses, sheep, and hogs."

A board of advisors was suggested to encourage all persons to destroy the animals named. The board would pay the bounties on the pelts of such animals. The bounties would be fifty cents for a small wolf and three dollars for a large wolf. Two dollars would be paid for a bearskin and five dollars for the skin of a panther.

After the report was accepted, it was moved and seconded that money be raised for the payment of bounties. It was moved and seconded that Indians might collect the bounty, too, and that the bounty of a child be paid to the parent.

Every motion was passed without question. With sighs of satisfaction, the voters leaned back. Were there any more resolutions to be offered which would guarantee the future security of the farmyard animals?

There was one more thing. Joe Meek nudged Ambrose as a man rose to his feet, an American.

"We have done a worthy thing today, gentlemen," the man said warmly. "We have provided a just and natural protection for our animals.

"But how is it with you and me and our children and wives? Have we any organization upon which we can rely for our own protection? Is there any power in the country which will protect us and all we hold dear on earth? Who is empowered to call us together to protect our lives and the lives of our families as we have now protected the livestock?

"I move the adoption of the following resolution that we may have protection for ourselves, as well as for cattle and herds: Resolved that a committee be appointed to consider the measures for the civil and military welfare of this colony."

There was a long moment of breath-held silence. Who would do more to protect his cattle than to protect human life? Who could vote "yes" to one and "no" to the other resolution?

Solemnly, the resolution was accepted. A committee of twelve was named to select the method of government best suited to Oregon's need for security.

Swayed by good humor and a feeling of friendliness, the Canadians shook hands and slapped American shoulders. No more wolf trouble, eh? No more running out to the farmyard barefoot at night. No more howls from wild beasts in the corrals. Everything was very fine.

But as the Canadians ambled down to the canoes, homeward-bound, a few were frowning doubtfully. The weather-beaten faces of old voyageurs were beginning to reflect a disturbing question. Exactly what had they committed themselves to? And what would the factor, Dr. McLoughlin, say when he learned that they had voted "yes" to a motion for government?

CHAPTER 14
Challenge at Champoeg

"There is only one thing to do," advised John McLoughlin sternly. "Get out every British vote for the final meeting called for May. Vote 'no.'" Vote "no," as they always should have done. When the Committee of Twelve made its report, the Canadians must vote "no" to every resolution, no matter how harmless it seemed.

The situation was not quite so black as the Hudson's Bay Company leaders had thought at first. Foolish though the Canadians' vote had been, it brought the question of American and British claims sharply to attention. Only a *study* of government had been approved. When the study was presented, it would be American in spirit. Its defeat by British votes would prove plainly and for all the world that British claims were stronger than American in Oregon.

"Yes," advised the Company factor. "Vote. Get every man to vote, but see that he votes 'no.'"

The friendliness that had ruled the wolf meeting was gone. The Committee of Twelve met and studied and debated. They learned the Iowa code of laws backward and forward. They quarreled among themselves over whether or not Oregon should have a governor. The Canadians grew increasingly uneasy. The Americans were a little alarmed by the importance of what they had begun. Now they saw, too, that it was all or nothing, win or lose, when they came together to vote.

Louis Palette showed his feelings by demanding the return of the red cow. He had left it through the winter so that Debbie might have milk to drink. Now, he said, he would give the tricky Americans no kindness. He would take the cow or shoot it.

Tackett couldn't see the animal killed. He offered to drive it home for Louis. As he herded the longhorn through the woods, Louis swaggered beside him. Keeping a wary eye on the cow, the little Canadian boasted of the defeat he and his friends meant to give the move for provisional government.

"Pa says we can't lose," countered Tackett. "There are more Americans in the valley than Britishers. We'll have government, and you'll support it, as you agreed to."

"I agreed, yes, if most people decide for government. But most will not," Louis said with such certainty that Tackett began to wonder.

Joe Meek, too, thought that the Canadians were more confident than was natural. Suddenly they wore grins and winks instead of worried looks. Before the wolf meetings, the Americans had felt and shown such secret happiness. Now the Company men were the ones who looked pleased. "By the great shaggy mountain," Joe muttered, "the Canadians have got some foxy trick up their sleeves."

The meeting date was set for the 2nd of May, and the place was named as the Hudson's Bay Company granary at Champoeg. After the steady rains, the sky had cleared, and the weather promised its fairest face for the important day. But the river was rising rapidly, and the Canadians looked at it and smiled.

On the morning of the meeting day, Ambrose looked out and frowned. "The creek's over its banks, and the river will be higher still," he said to Tackett. "I don't think you and Debbie ought to risk the trip to Champoeg. I wouldn't go myself if it weren't so important."

"We've got to go," protested Tackett. "It—it's just as important to us as it is to you, even if we can't vote. We're American, too!"

"American," Debbie coaxed. "American, Pa?"

The father's face softened as he looked down at her. Truly it would be a day they would long remember. Even though Debbie wouldn't be staying here to grow up in Oregon, she could boast that she had been present when its government was born.

"Very well," he said. "But I'll handle the skiff myself."

They were up before daybreak on the great day. Ambrose was so nervous he pulled a button off his good coat while trying to fasten it, and Tackett had to hunt the needle and a scrap of thread to sew it on. His hands were shaking, too. He had seen Louis Palette spryly paddling past in his canoe. As he streaked by, Louis had pointed his clenched fist at their cabin as if he was prepared to defy the whole American settlement.

"They're bound they'll win," Tack said in a worried voice.

"They can't," Ambrose said firmly. "We are certain of sixty-five votes, at least ten more than the Britishers have."

Sixty-five—mountain men, farmers, and missionaries—surely that would be enough to win!

The landing at Champoeg was already crowded with canoes, dugouts, skiffs, and even a small sailing schooner. Ambrose edged his skiff in carefully to the bank and looked back at the swollen, flooded river. "That's a bad threat to travelers," he remarked. "I wonder if Joe Meek made it safely."

"I'd have got here if I had to swim," Joe shouted, leaning over the bank. "Toss up that pretty little girl in the red cape."

Debbie kicked her heels as the big man hoisted her to shore. She clapped her hands with joy as she caught sight of Keetow and Mrs. Garret.

"I wouldn't have missed it!" cried Mrs. Garret. "I'll have great news to carry home."

Tackett shut his ears to that unhappy reminder and let Keetow take charge of Debbie while he joined the boys and men. The little town was a turmoil of people. It was a holiday, but underneath the gaiety was a hard fighting spirit among Americans and Company men alike.

Webb Heathwire ran by, his rough hair on end. "Come on!" he yelled. "We're goin' to get them Company boys."

Tackett grabbed at his arm. "No, you don't! This is to be a peaceable vote."

"Peaceable!" Webb blurted. He stared at Tackett, then looked away. "Well, iffen you say so, Tack."

Joe Meek, wearing his white satin vest, was striding from group to group, taking a roll call of the Americans. "Where's Jason Lee?" he asked. "Didn't he come with the bunch from the Mission?"

Lee was not there, nor was George Abernathy. The leaders of the Mission had decided to stay away from political action. They had the welfare of the Mission to consider. That made two less votes than the Americans had expected to count.

But other settlers were missing, too. Joe's face got longer and longer as he searched vainly for this one or that. Time for the meeting was drawing near. There were no more boats in sight on the river, and at least a dozen American votes were missing—mostly settlers far up the river.

"What happened?" worried Ambrose. "I can't believe that all of them mean to stay away."

Louis Palette swaggered up, grinning knowingly. "Maybe your friends come some other day," he remarked. "Maybe nex' week they come to vote."

"They know this is the day. Everyone's been told."

"I think somebody give word meeting is postpone because of river flood," chuckled Louis happily. "No use look for them today."

Joe crushed one big fist into the other. "They done it!" he groaned. "By the Great Beaver, they foxed us, Ambrose. We've lost the vote before it's took!"

The doors of the granary were opened wide; there could be no more delay. In the dusty, dim room, the Committee of Twelve was already seated, nervously clutching papers. They were trying to count, as everyone else was doing, the number of friends and of enemies.

Women and children were not allowed inside—there was scarcely room for all the men—but windows and doors were left opened so that those outside might hear the proceedings. Tackett hoisted Debbie to a window ledge and made room for Mrs. Garret and Keetow beside him. In the stillness that had caught the crowd, he heard the chairman, the Reverend Babcock, call the meeting to order.

The chairman asked, "Mr. Le Breton, will you read us the report of the Committee?" The secretary got slowly to his feet.

"I will," he said. Paper rustled in his shaking hand, and he cleared his throat twice, then read loudly:

"The Committee has found that it is advisable to organize ourselves into a civil community. The provisional government so provided will bring law and order until such time as the United States will extend its jurisdiction over us. For this purpose we suggest that the voters select a sheriff and other necessary officers. We also suggest that they appoint a committee of nine to write a code of laws and officers to head a militia."

Le Breton had scarcely lifted his eyes from the report when a settler moved that it be accepted. Stamping feet, whistles, and shouts drowned the chairman's voice as he asked for a vote by a show of hands.

It was impossible to count. Men wouldn't stand still; they milled around, shouting, arguing. Some held two hands high, while others knocked their neighbors' hands down. Two big men blocked off a smaller man so his vote could not be seen.

"Gentlemen, I am unable to decide!" cried Babcock.

"Those in favor of the report, please say 'aye.' Those opposed, say 'no.'"

The "ayes" rose deafeningly, but they came from outside as well as inside the building. Boys and women were helping the vote. The Indian wives of the Canadians caught the spirit and added a loud "no" to their husbands' voices. Once more the chairman protested.

"Hurrah! We win!" cried a Canadian, and all at once the meeting seemed to break up. Men turned to the open doors and surged out into the sunshine. The chairman and members of the committee followed helplessly. They tried to hold the meeting in order, crying that the vote had not yet been properly counted.

"Line them up out here and count them!" cried Ambrose.

"Yes," agreed Le Breton. "We can risk it. Let us divide and count."

"Second the motion!" called a settler.

Their words were lost in the turmoil. The Canadians were dancing and hugging each other; they were certain that victory was theirs. Then suddenly, a great voice rang through the crowded street of Champoeg and echoed over the river.

"Who's for a divide! Who's for a divide! All in favor of the report and an organization, follow me!"

Joe Meek stepped out, his hand held high. Everyone turned to stare at him; quickly the American members of the committee fell in line with him. Others followed, scrambling for places, pulling the slow ones with them.

The Canadians hesitated, looked at one another questioningly, then shrugged and hurried to make their own line. They weren't afraid of a vote. They had counted their men.

Suddenly there was a stir. A man was in the wrong line—here was Etienne Lucier with the Americans. It had been thought that only Francois Mathieu, the newcomer, was in favor of government.

Louis Palette rushed to drag his friend back, to put him where he belonged, among those voting "no." Etienne struggled. He stood half way between the two lines, arguing with Louis and with Francois Mathieu. Louis held Etienne on one side. Francois gripped his other arm; their voices rose loud and angry. Except for those three, everyone else was in line.

Tackett had been counting the American line. Keetow was counting the Canadian. Keetow whispered, "Fifty Canadians!"

Tackett gulped. "There's fifty in our line, too!"

It was a tie, with Etienne Lucier and Francois Mathieu still arguing it out in the middle. Louis Palette had loosed his grip and stepped back angrily to the Canadian line.

Lucier nodded, thrust out his hand to Mathieu, then turned with him to give his vote to the report. The tie was broken. Provisional government under the flag of the United States had begun in Oregon.

Joe Meek's yell shook the ancient oaks and split the blue skies. His was the loudest among many cheers. Never had there been such excitement in old Champoeg!

Tackett hugged Debbie so hard she cried out in protest. Mrs. Garret tried to hug all three children at once. "Isn't it wonderful! Isn't it wonderful!" she kept saying. "Oh, I'm so proud of your father!"

Joe Meek's hat went sailing high in the air. With Ambrose, he came pushing through the crowd. To right and left he was announcing that he was running for the office of sheriff. He was glowing with good humor. Ambrose, too, looked happier than Tackett had seen him since they reached Oregon. He stood straighter, and his eyes had more sparkle than ever before.

"We're on our way to Statehood," he said. "Think of that, boy!"

Mrs. Garret thrust a hand to each of the men. "I'm so proud of you," she said. "Of both of you."

Joe Meek looked at her pink, smiling face, and then he looked at Ambrose. He put the hand he was holding with the one that Ambrose held. "Ma'am, you better not leave Oregon," he said. "There's a man and his family that needs you here, and the country needs you, too."

"Why, Mr. Meek!" Anne Garret gasped. She tried to snatch her hands away, but Ambrose held them fast.

"Joe said it for me, Anne," he said. "But it's been in my heart—only waiting to be spoken. Will you stay with us in Oregon? Will you be my wife?"

Her face flushed to the color of an Oregon rose. Her gaze was fixed on the two hands holding hers. "Keetow," she whispered. "I can't give up Keetow."

"You won't need to, Anne. She'll be our child, just as Tackett and Debbie are."

She turned to the three children—to the wide-eyed Indian girl, the boy who looked almost afraid to hope, and the yellow-haired baby who clung to her skirts. No need to ask what they wanted her to do.

Two tears came to her eyes, and her mouth trembled. "Yes, Ambrose," she said, "I'll be happy to be your wife."

It was the best part of a perfect day, thought Tackett. There was such joy in him he almost expected to burst with it. Keetow and Mrs. Garret were crying for no reason on earth he could see. His father was wildly shaking hands with everyone near him, and Debbie was turning cartwheels. Tackett didn't know what he could do to show his excitement. Then he saw Webb Heathwire over by the oak trees in a crowd of wrestling boys.

"Get up, Webb!" he shouted, running toward him. "Get up here now, and I'll show you that hold."

THE END

More Books from The Good and the Beautiful Library

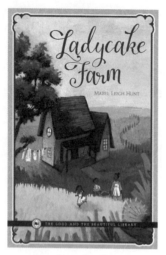

Ladycake Farm
by Mabel Leigh Hunt

Jade Dragons
by Florence Wightman Rowland

Redwood Pioneer
by Betty Stirling

Trini, the Strawberry Girl
by Johanna Spyri

goodandbeautiful.com